Ladies Who Lust

A Mischief Collection of Erotica

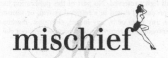

mischief

Mischief
An imprint of HarperCollins*Publishers*
77–85 Fulham Palace Road,
Hammersmith, London W6 8JB

www.mischiefbooks.com

A Paperback Original 2013

First published in Great Britain in ebook format by
HarperCollins*Publishers* 2012

Copyright
Marmalade © Delilah Devlin
Barmaids © Lara Lancey
Drama Queen © Heather Towne
Letting Go © Lucy Lush
A Taste of London © Chrissie Bentley
No Strings Attached © Elizabeth Coldwell
Whore-Maker © Scarlett Rush
I Obey Her © Valerie Grey
Beach Scene © Primula Bond

The author asserts the moral right to
be identified as the author of this work

A catalogue record for this book is
available from the British Library

ISBN-13: 978-0-00-755315-0

Find out more about HarperCollins and the environment at
www.harpercollins.co.uk/green

CONTENTS

Contents

Marmalade
Delilah Devlin

The invitation was unexpected. And, in my opinion, unearned. My husband Greg was new to Talbot Enterprises and there were several layers of management between himself and Bob Talbot, the President and CEO. Greg had barely finished the company's rigid orientation and had just begun to join the seasoned legal eagles in their annual policy reviews to acclimate to the corporate culture.

Still, the prissy vellum envelope lay on my belly where Greg had dropped it as soon as he'd swept into the bedroom, proof of this unexpected turn. His face was ruddy from excitement and the run up the stairs to our third-storey apartment. I felt like The Grinch for letting my naturally suspicious nature question a windfall – a chance for Greg to spend some time alone with the boss and cultivate a valuable relationship.

'Why do you suppose he asked us?' I sat up, a bit perturbed that he was much more excited about the invitation to spend a weekend at the Talbots' lodge than to find me nude and wearing clamps on my nipples, and my pussy shaved and glistening with opal glitter. However, I wasn't about to spoil his moment of triumph simply because I was horny, and therefore grumpy. 'Are you sure we're the only other couple going to Cedar Lake this weekend?'

Greg didn't answer because his glance had snagged at last on my glittering pussy. He nearly strangled himself yanking off his tie. Buttons pinged against the floor as he wrestled his way out of his dress shirt.

To forestall permanent injury to the treasure in his trousers, I reached for his buckle, tugged it open and jerked down his fly.

He was balls-deep before he said, 'We'll be the only couple there for the whole fucking weekend.' His head swooped down, and he kissed me hard. 'Up for it?'

What's a girl gonna say when her hubby's whole body is taut with excitement, and that's saying a lot because he worked out to maintain his former linebacker physique?

I shoved aside my doubts, dug my nails into his ass and said, 'Why not? Sounds like fun, babe.'

* * *

I'd first met Tess Talbot at a corporate wives tea. She'd presided over the gathering, wearing a white silk suit that moulded her lush curves, her platinum hair twisted into a neat bun. I'd been intimidated by the formality of the event – too many utensils and fragile porcelain – and by her stature. She was tall and shaped like Charlize Theron while I was built more like the little girl in Juno.

Further, she was very, very British – her diction crisply precise. I had to watch every word to keep from dropping 'g's and sounding like a hick.

At the tea, she'd been gracious, her glance taking in my girlish sheath dress without a curve to mar the straight lines. Even then, I'd imagined she'd been about to say something. Maybe a kindly suggestion to never wear yellow, or to tell me I had strawberry jam on my chin, something I'd discovered when I'd hit the ladies' room later.

Now standing in the living room of their 'little lodge', a monstrous log and limestone house which towered over Cedar Lake, I still felt like a little brown mouse beside her luminous, moonlight-coloured dress and stunning face.

Greg's arms slipped around my waist from behind and pulled me close to rub his crotch against my backside. Ever since he'd come back from sharing cigars on the veranda with Bob, he'd been downright giddy.

I slapped his arm. 'Behave,' I whispered, turning my head to deliver a mock frown. 'Your boss is watching us.'

He laughed and nuzzled the side of my neck. 'He doesn't mind, baby.' He bit my earlobe, then chuckled. 'His wife is into you.'

I froze, my glance sliding to Tess, who stood beside Bob. Her husband's hand rested on her hip, and he was leaning toward her ear as well, but whispering. Both of the Talbots stared directly at me.

'What do you mean?' I said, sure I'd misheard or that he was teasing me. He knew how uncomfortable I was. I'd been mostly mute throughout dinner while the men talked about work and the Texas political scene. Tess had chimed in a time or two, but for the most part had watched me much like a cat ready to pounce on a furry little rodent.

'Haven't you noticed that she hasn't stopped staring all evening?' Greg whispered in my ear. 'I thought she'd reach across the table to pinch your nipple when you sat down. You almost fell out of that dress.'

I blushed. I'd found the dress in a local gift shop just that day but, as always, while it fitted snugly through the torso, my meagre breasts failed to fill out the top. 'It's the best I could do on short notice when I ran to town after lunch. Their invitation said it was a "casual weekend". I wasn't expecting to dress for dinner.'

Greg gave my cheek a smacking kiss then released me. 'I'm telling you she's not worried about the fact the dress doesn't fit,' he murmured. 'Your nipples are hard. It's hard not to stare.'

4

A flush of heat, not all of it due to embarrassment, crept from my cheeks to my chest. The tips of my nipples grew long when they were excited. Greg called them 'stems'. Because of the low neckline and the fact the dress dipped low in the back as well, I hadn't been able to wear a bra. My nipples poked at the front of the dress.

'It's cold in here,' I said, wrapping my arms over my chest.

'Sure it is,' he murmured. 'But she's not looking because she thinks you should've worn a bra. Bob hinted that his wife likes a playmate for these weekends.'

'So I'm along to entertain her?' I drew a deep breath. 'You know I'm not good at small talk.'

Greg snorted. 'You weren't just "not good" tonight – you sucked. You've hardly said a word to her all evening. You're never this tense.'

It was true, but I hoped he put my silence down to fatigue. The drive from Austin to the Talbots' lakeside lodge had been a long one and, despite the air conditioning, I felt wilted inside and out. The last thing I wanted him to guess was that I had a major girl-crush on the boss's wife. Inappropriate, much?

Greg gave me a wink. 'Don't worry about tonight. We all had a long drive. Bob and I are hittin' the golf course in the morning. It'll just be you girls. You'll have a chance to get to know each other.'

'I'm sure we'll be bosom buddies,' I muttered.

Greg laughed. 'Yeah, about that … I have the feeling she's interested in more than talkin' about the next ladies' tea.'

'What are you sayin'?'

He arched a brow, devilment glittering in his dark eyes. 'Just that I won't consider it cheatin' – but I do get to hear all the dirty details.'

I scoffed. 'Stop teasing. They'll hear.'

'Baby, I'm tellin' you, she's the one who put the bug in the boss's ear to get us here. She's the one who made our golf date. Miz Talbot's been checkin' out your boobs and ass all evening. I think she wants you.'

I shook my head, my cheeks on fire. But I couldn't deny something else was just as hot – now when I squirmed, rubbing my thighs together.

'All the dirty details,' he whispered.

God, I loved him.

* * *

Dressed in a silk robe I'd found on a hook behind the bathroom door, I sat at the breakfast table with Tess. We waved through the window at the men as they climbed into Bob's Beemer. The men smiled. Greg gave a waggle of his eyebrows, and then they were gone.

When my gaze returned to her, she smiled like the Cheshire cat. 'This is nice,' she said peering at me over the rim of her teacup. 'Just us girls. How ever will we entertain ourselves?'

I bit the corner of my lip, a blush beginning to heat my cheeks, because she looked like a movie star, and her robe had parted, revealing a deep, luscious décolletage. I had a weakness for lovely bosoms, something Greg indulged with the porno flicks he brought home, featuring generously endowed women.

Tess set her cup in her saucer and leaned over the table. 'Do you mind doing something for me?'

My glance darted up from her chest. Since Greg had been so adamant about his suspicions, I already had an inkling what would happen this day. I nodded, hoping my husband hadn't been dead wrong. 'What do you have in mind, Tess?' I asked, keeping my expression open and innocent.

Her lush mouth pursed. 'I thought we might get to know each other. You're really very lovely. So petite. I couldn't help noticing. Do you mind opening your robe, my dear? I've been dying to see your breasts.'

I cleared my throat. 'My breasts. You want to see them?'

'Yes, dear. *Now.*'

My nipples tingled, beginning to slowly ripen. 'Um, is my husband's job at risk?' I asked, my voice small and breathy. I glanced up from beneath my eyelashes, letting her know this was part of the game, something that pleased me, pretending reluctance because I wanted my sexual partner to be in charge.

Her mouth twitched then flattened. Her chin rose to a haughty angle. 'You don't have to do a thing, my dear. However, you should know that when I'm pleased, so is Bob.'

'Oh.' I sank my teeth into my lower lip and let my gaze slide away. Then holding my breath, I leaned back in my seat and eased aside the lapels of the floral silk robe, one side at a time, holding the belt closed to preclude a view of anything farther south. The lapels framed my breasts. 'They're small,' I said, feeling like I should apologise.

'Your nipples aren't.' She rose in her seat and reached across to tug on a lengthening stem.

I hadn't expected her to be quite that bold. I drew in a deep, jagged breath. Arousal bloomed, dampening my pussy and likely leaving a wet spot beneath me. From her hard challenging stare, I didn't think she'd mind.

Her fingertips tightened painfully on my nipple, and she pulled, drawing me off my chair and around the table until I bent over her, breasts level with her mouth. She turned her seat to face me, then leaned forward and tongued the other nipple, which already protruded.

Everything was happening so fast, all I could do was react. All thoughts of how I must look or sound flew out of my head. I gasped and whimpered as she twisted the one nipple and lavished its twin with succulent tugs and wicked flicks. My nipples drew tighter, dimpling, the tips elongating. Glancing down, I loved the way her mouth sucked on one of them like a straw, drawing so hard I felt the pull all the way to my cunt. I grasped the arms of her chair and arched my back to thrust my breasts closer, mashing the one she suckled against her face.

Her chuckle was muffled and dry. When she pulled back, she raised a brow. 'It's quite warm in here. You don't really need that robe, do you?' she said, pinching both my nipples hard.

I glanced out the window, at the long manicured lawn and the lakeshore that rimmed the edge. There wasn't a soul around to see me as I eagerly shimmied out of the robe, letting it puddle on the floor behind me. I clasped my hands in front of my pussy, assuming a modest stance.

Her gaze raked my body, lingering on my pussy before coming back to my face. 'You're pretty. I can see why Greg dotes. Do you lead him around by your pretty cunt?'

I was shocked by her words, but not disgusted. Pleasure melted from inside me, glazing my inner thighs. 'I like him taking the lead,' I said softly, then, even softer still, I added, 'I like it even better when he forces me to do … things.'

She nodded crisply and let go of my tit. Her back stiffened as she faced forward again, pushed her dishes away, then tapped the table top in front of her. 'Lie on the table, legs spread in front of me. I like a little marmalade on my muffin.'

Dazed by the hard, commanding note in her voice, I found myself backing up to the table, giving a little hop that jiggled my buttocks. Then I lifted my legs and scooted toward her. Centred, I peered at her set expression through my parted legs and placed my feet on her chair's armrests. Her features remained neutral, her eyes narrowed. Not until I was staring at the ceiling did I realise how eager I was, how completely and deliciously she dominated me.

Cool gel landed on my mound, and I glanced down to where she spooned apple jelly onto my pussy – two large spoonfuls, which she proceeded to distribute with her long, tapered fingers. Sticky jelly cooled my swelling outer lips.

'I like that it's bare,' she said, her voice uninflected. Then she bent and stuck out her tongue to lick at the mess she'd made. 'I love jam on a hot, toasted muffin.'

I bit back a smile, then jerked when she bit one lip. My pussy contracted. The point of her tongue burrowed into my entrance, and I forced myself to relax. She entered me, swirling inside and continuing to spread and demolish the cool jelly with efficient flicks and swipes.

Her hands flattened on my inner thighs, and I realised I'd held them tensed until she forced them down. Fully open, wonderfully vulnerable, I lay on my back, thighs splayed as Tess bent over me, fully savouring her meal.

Gone was the spoon. She thrust two fingers into the jelly and painted my labia again, then pushed the two taloned digits inside me.

'Oh!' I gasped, wondering at the proper etiquette. Should I moan? Thrash? Should I come? That question became more urgent as her fingers swirled, and her lips began to nibble at my clitoris. 'Tess?'

'Mmmm?' she said, thrusting and sucking, her face disappearing from view.

Lord, I was nearly done, overcome with the tension coiling deep inside my belly. I glanced out the window and had one last thought for any passers-by. 'Tess!' I came up on my elbows, and she slowly raised her head.

Her mouth was covered in glistening jelly. Her lips were reddened, swollen as my cunt. 'You shouldn't rest your elbows on the table, dear.'

She was lecturing me on manners? 'Tess, I … can we take the *jelly* somewhere else?'

Her smile stretched across her face. 'I've just the spot.'

The 'spot' was hers and Bob's bed. 'The sheets will be a mess,' I said, trailing behind her, jelly sticking to my thighs.

'Not to worry. Bob and I often eat in bed,' she said and gave a bark of laughter. 'Now lie down, but don't get too comfortable. Can't have you nodding off.'

As if. I lay back, instantly opening my legs, waiting impatiently as Tess peeled off her robe and let it drop. She stood still for a moment to let me look.

She was perfectly formed. Breasts as large as melons, nipples a creamy, satiny beige. Her belly was taut, her hips full. Her pussy – I licked my lips, because hers was smooth as well, her inner lips a pink fringe that protruded from between smallish outer labia.

'Now, now, I know you barely touched your breakfast.' Tess crawled onto the bed beside me, then tipped the jelly jar and stuck her fingers inside. This time, she smoothed it over her own bare pussy. When she side-stepped over me and settled her pussy above my mouth, I didn't mind, because hers was already buried between my legs.

While she slathered my cunt with wet open-mouthed kisses and spike-tongued flutters, I munched on hers, finding her smallish lips a tasty treat as I licked her clean from clit to asshole, then settled in to suck that pretty pink fringe. I smoothed the jelly with a fingertip, working it upward until I rubbed it onto her small puckered hole. Her body quivered above me. Her knees widened, giving me greater access.

We were so in tune. Our mouths slowed and sipped, lashed and bit in unison, fingers plunging into ass and cunt with wild abandon.

Again, I approached the precipice, cunt clenching around her fingers, my hips pulsing up and down. 'Tess?'

'Go, already,' she groaned, her voice muffled, her enunciation less than precise. 'I'm holding on by a bloody thread here, girl,' she gasped. 'By all means, come!'

My hips popped, lifting her with my powerful swells. Her pussy lowered, grinding against my mouth and tongue. I breathed noisily through my nostrils, but flicked my tongue at her clit as she was doing to mine, until the spiral broke, and I arched, fingers digging into her round ass.

Moments later, I recovered to find her body slumped atop mine, my chin cupped against her pussy. I laughed, and she stirred with a moan.

'Do you think the boys enjoyed themselves half as much today?' I asked, my voice lazy and happy because I was still riding a euphoric high.

Tess pushed up, then backed away, her pussy then the tender undersides of her large breasts disappearing from view. 'If they're lucky, they might find another jar of jam in the fridge when they return.'

My eyes widened.

Tess snickered. 'It isn't cheating if all they do is watch.'

* * *

Greg goose-stepped me up the stairs, a hand cupping my elbow to hurry me along. Once we passed the door, he kicked it shut.

I backed away, deliberately scuffling toward the bed, although I kept my eyes wide and my bottom lip quivering. 'You're frightening me,' I said, although he really

13

wasn't. His arms were tangled in his short-sleeved shirt as he wrestled it over his head. When it cleared, he tossed it to the floor, then strode toward me, evil intent in his narrowed gaze. 'She said I had to,' I whined, 'that your job was on the line.'

His hands reached for me, and he whirled me around and bent me over the side of the bed. 'Imagine my shock and disgust – my wife with her ass in the air, her nasty pussy exposed for my employer to see – and covered in strawberry jelly!'

A slap landed on my buttocks, and I groaned and tried to twist away, but he held me down with a hand at the centre of my back as he spanked me several more times.

My ass warmed as he punished me with firm swats across both buttocks before centring sharper, quicker slaps on my hot pussy. 'I was humiliated,' he said cheerfully. 'I don't know how I'll hold up my head.'

I giggled, but the next swat landed so hard against my wet flesh that my gaping hole suctioned on his palm as he pulled away. His hand rubbed me there, then fingers thrust straight into my sticky pussy. 'And worse, there's no jam left for tomorrow's breakfast.'

I'd have laughed, but didn't have the breath. Fingers worked in and out, and his other hand moved from my back. I came up on my elbows and glanced behind me just as he knelt and burrowed his face into my sopping folds.

14

'Tess enjoyed herself,' I said. 'She's got quite the appetite ... for *mahrm-a-lahd*,' I said, stretching my vowels
to mimic her accent.

'I've got quite an appetite myself,' Greg growled. Then
he thrust three fingers inside my dripping channel and
twisted his hand, screwing them in deeper.

I tilted my ass higher, the scent of apples, strawberries,
and the lingering tease of Tess's lovely sea-fresh pussy
wafting in the air. 'Tell me. Did Bob see me?'

'Mmmm?' Greg vibrated, but didn't lift his head to
say more.

'Do you think he liked seeing me eating his muffin?'

Greg bit my clit, then thrust a fourth finger inside
me, pushing in and pulling out. 'He likes your appetite.
I fear we'll be spending many more dreadfully boring
weekends here on the lake.'

I smiled, laying my face on the coverlet and enjoying
the pull of the fabric on the jam stuck to my cheeks.
When Greg replaced his hand with his cock, I floated in
a happy, lusty haze, imagining the next time Tess and I
would munch on each others' goodies ... savouring the
taste of muffins and marmalade.

Barmaids
Lara Lancey

The rooftop bar overlooked Madison Avenue but inside it was done out like the library of a stately home. Bottle-green book-lined walls, beaten-up leather Chesterfield sofas and chairs, low-lit lamps and candles, and, to top it all, a roaring log fire. The best of both worlds, really. It may have been fake, but it was still a corner of good old England tucked above the glittering streets of New York.

And best of all my business here was all done. I was free to relax. Yes, it was a slight nuisance that my flight back to London was delayed for a couple of days by the worst snow the east coast had experienced in decades, but hey. Other people were paying for my time, let alone my air fare, so what was the rush? There was no one waiting at Heathrow waving a placard. The office were eager to fête my successful snaring of an interview with the new

Brad Pitt on the block, but we'd already communicated most of the excitement over Skype.

And where better to be stranded than in the city that never sleeps?

I found a big armchair by the fire and crossed one leg over the other with a swish of stocking. My legs looked too long, and exposed, in the firelight. I still wasn't used to wearing this working uniform. I felt like I was playing dress-up. They'd all warned me that women in New York were impeccably dressed and groomed, especially in the publicity business, and they were right. The jeans and biker jackets had been left behind in my flat in Long Acre and here I was, zipped into a grey Chanel suit and a flimsy pussy-bow blouse.

I was sitting too close to the fire, and my skin was prickling up with the heat. I ran my finger round the collar of my blouse to cool myself. The creamy lace of my camisole tickled the surface of my skin as I fanned myself, and was swallowed into my deep cleavage as I sighed. I took a long swallow of my white wine, glanced down and noticed that my skirt had ridden up too high, exposing an inch or so of flesh above the stocking top. I was about to tug at my skirt when I thought better of it. The sight of my own pale thigh had stirred me. Perhaps I shouldn't have ordered a second glass. I liked seeing the firm white skin exposed there. It made my stomach sizzle.

I left the lace stocking top showing. One or two of the men by the bar had finally noticed me, and had turned to stare at my legs. No doubt imagining the promise of what lay just under my skirt – my silky knickers, and then the secret nestling between my thighs. I read somewhere that men like stockings because they make the legs look bare, vulnerable, yet make them a brazen gateway, or pathway, straight up to the cunt.

My smile grew wider. Perhaps I could do what I'd always fantasised about, especially so far from home. Pull a gorgeous stranger in Manhattan, shag him senseless in his loft apartment somewhere near here until the sun came up, then do all the things they do in movies like sit in shiny diners eating waffles, walk in Central Park, get windblown on the Staten Island ferry, eat some more from a hot-dog vendor, go dancing, back to his for more crazy fucking in front of a huge plate-glass window so millions of other penthouse people could see, then go home flying the flag for English girls. Hell, it had been over a year since I'd had sex, and thanks to this job I'd had a total makeover and felt pretty hot. I was more than up for it, especially with another couple of Sauvignons inside me.

I swung my foot gently, so that the sliver of flesh between skirt and stocking stretched and shrank with the movement. I refused to catch anyone's eye just yet.

An ice blonde with cropped hair, teetering silver

heels and a minuscule sequinned dress appeared in the doorway. She was all alone, and surveyed the half-empty room, presumably looking for her date. I thought her glance fell on me, but with the hall light behind her all I could see was a kind of devilish glitter in her eyes, and anyway I would have been a disappointment

She walked just like Charlize Theron in the *J'Adore* advert, where she's sashaying through a Paris apartment pulling off her dress and her pearls. She swayed straight up to the bar and sat down confidently on a tall stool. As the barman leaned across to take her order the girl slowly crossed her legs Sharon Stone style and I noticed with a thump of shock that she wasn't wearing any knickers. The quick flash of pink slit was unmistakeable. Why hadn't I thought of that?

Her long fingers swizzled the cocktail the guy had given her, then she turned and her eyes locked on to me again. She tipped her head upwards in a kind of greeting. Or invitation.

There was a dampness across my upper lip now. I really was too hot. I stood up, feeling the leather seat of my chair sticking to my damp skin. I was desperate just to throw the jacket right off so that I could cool myself. I grasped the lapels, ready to do it. She was still watching me. I had a mad urge to strip, to really surprise her, and make the scattering of sombre men wake up at the sight of my bare breasts, invite them to touch me, do more to me if they chose.

But I closed the lapels again, breathing hard, trying to ignore the nipples stiffening against the jacket lining. Don't be daft. Be discreet. I repeated this mantra. *Don't be daft, be discreet.* It would be a good title for my next article. And it summed up the two halves of my personality. Up until now I had crashed through life dressed like a boy and was totally daft. But now I was doing the job I'd always craved, in a city I'd always dreamed about, and I had to be discreet. If I played my cards right at the magazine there was the possibility of a permanent relocation to New York.

A central switch suddenly dimmed the lighting even more, and some low, jazzy music came on. The barman seemed to be in charge of the ambience, if it was he who had dimmed the lighting. He was deep in conversation with the girl. Perhaps he was her date. Or perhaps she'd asked him to change the mood.

I was hot, I was thirsty again, and for some reason I must have been nervous, because my heart was pounding. I walked up to the bar. The barman was serving a group of older women at the far end, and the ice blonde was still there on her chair, still alone. She glanced at me. Up close her eyes had the depth and facets of a pale-blue diamond. Her glance travelled on down the front of my blouse, button by button. Then she glanced away, twisting the stem of her glass. One foot swung idly, dangling its spiked stiletto.

I drummed my fingers on the chrome, trying to attract the attention of the barman. But the cougars weren't going to let him go. One of them had her bejewelled hand on his wrist as if to trap him, and was slipping a piece of paper into his hand.

The icy blonde looked at me again. Her pale, frosted lips parted.

'Allow me.'

She hitched herself up onto the shiny bar, swung her legs over and dropped down on the other side. She started tossing the cocktail shakers around like a juggler, throwing ice, spouting colourful liquids, shaking them round her head and behind her back, and this was all for me. No one else was watching. It was just her and me, and then she was slamming two elegant glasses down on the bar.

'Daiquiri Delilah.' Her voice was husky, crackling with too many cigarettes, which made it quite manly. But the soft white breasts squeezed between her slender arms as she pushed the drink over to me were pure woman.

'Delilah?'

'My name.'

She was back up on the bar, and this time as she swung herself back over to my side I could see the full glory of her fully waxed pussy, the white sex lips gleaming like juicy scallops stripped of their shell, barely concealed in the slight shadow of her dress.

'And what's yours?'

There was the rough edge of a foreign accent in her voice. Nordic, I guessed. She chinked her glass against mine, and now our knees were touching as we sat face to face. Not a difficult question, but then again this was the one chance in my life to be totally anonymous. The freedom of it was hitting me, filling me with a dark excitement. I could tell her whatever I liked. Be whoever I liked. Let her befriend me, show me the city, show me her friends.

'I'm Clara.' OK, so I'd run out of original ideas. After all, I'm never going to see her again. I shrugged my jacket off and flung it onto the back of my stool. 'Thanks for the drink.'

The alcohol started to take hold, heating up my veins. I was going to loosen up, and enjoy myself. I bent my elbow to rest it on the bar. I drew my hand slowly inside the loose collar of my blouse and caressed my warm skin.

'You alone here in the States?' she asked, watching the way my hand was moving.

'Yeah. On business. And now I'm snowed in and can't get home.'

She nodded thoughtfully. 'You got somewhere to stay?'

If I had told her I was staying right here, at the Library Hotel, she wouldn't have to come to my rescue and there wouldn't be any adventure.

I shook my head and a shy blush rose perfectly

naturally to my cheeks. At the same time my fiddling fingertips brushed lower, onto my warm breast swelling under the flimsy camisole. She couldn't have missed it. This lightest of touches sent a bolt of excitement sizzling through me. I hadn't realised how horny the intimate, closed atmosphere of the bar – and the growing intensity between the two of us – had made me. Still looking at Delilah I spread my fingers over my breast under the camisole and when I felt my nipple perk up eagerly against the palm of my hand I slowly started to rub it.

Delilah's eyes flashed directly at what my hand was doing. She shifted on her chair and smiled. Her mouth was wide, her teeth a perfect white row. She started to mirror the action, except that her hand moved over the surface of her sparkly dress, tracing the small swell of her own breast.

'Why don't we get disgracefully drunk together and then later if you like I can show you the real New York,' she murmured, running her tongue over her lower lip in such an outrageously clichéd yet thoroughly sexy gesture that my pussy squeezed with longing and I could hear my breath rasping in my ears. 'I wouldn't want you to be all alone tonight.'

'Yes,' I answered thickly, pinching my nipple until it was hot.

'Yes to what?' she asked, dragging the cocktail shaker across and filling our glasses.

I glanced over my shoulder. The barman was still talking to the cougars, polishing the same wineglass over and over as if he had been hypnotised. The only other customers seemed to be a couple of businessmen drinking whisky in the corner.

'Yes please. To everything.'

She leaned a little closer, uncrossed her legs, and her white hand shot out and flipped undone the buttons on my blouse.

'So. No one's looking. Show me what you're doing to yourself, darling.'

My blouse had fallen softly open. She could see my hand, still lightly caressing my breast.

I sat up straighter, and ran my tongue across my dry mouth. 'Like this?'

'Oh yes, just like that. Now let me see you stroke the other one.'

I had some more to drink then lifted my hand, cold from the cocktail glass, to my other breast, and pushed them together. She hitched her stool closer to me so that her legs were on either side of mine, trapping me there, and she lifted my camisole right up so that my breasts, and my kneading hands, were exposed.

The music stopped briefly. The few beats of silence seemed endless. We both froze. Then it started again, a more rhythmic sound, heavy on the bass, and Delilah's tongue poked between her white teeth as her very long,

24

white fingers took my hands away from my breasts and pushed them down to rest on her thighs.

I felt tipsy, and hot, and helpless.

'What do you want me to do?'

'Touch me, Clara. You're so gorgeous, and I'm creaming myself here. I want you to touch me.'

My hands slid up her thighs, under the little dress, and rested on the crease at the top. I didn't know what to do next, but my God, she'd started something. There was a devil hopping about inside me. And the fact that there were other people here, who could turn and see what was happening at any moment and see two women mesmerised by each other, about to do incredible things to each other, that just excited me more.

She didn't rush me. She let me rest my hands there on her thighs, my fingers spreading open, treading on her, testing the feel of her skin, the give of her flesh, while she pulled my blouse right off me and ripped the camisole easily to one side. There was unveiled lust in her eyes now. My breasts bounced out. Both nipples were dark-red points, sore with the rubbing against my camisole and intoxicated with the soreness.

Her hands came up and slowly they came towards me, and when they touched my breasts it was so electrifying I nearly leaped out of my skin with shocked pleasure, pushing my body into her hands, arching my back to offer her my breasts. I tried to inch my bar stool closer with my feet hooked round the bars, but my knickers were stuck to the seat, my sticky pussy rubbing through the silk against the leather. I rubbed myself harder and there was the shock again, hotter this time, urging for more. My tight skirt rode further and further up until the stocking tops and then my knickers were plainly visible.

She pretended not to notice. Instead she squeezed my breasts and pinched my nipples harder, and then suddenly she leaned forward, balanced herself with her hands on either side of me, and took one nipple between her white teeth.

I thought I was going to go mad. She bit the nipple really hard, making me squeal with the pain, but it was gloriously wicked and I started to push against her face as she bit me then started to suck me, and the movement still had me rubbing against the leather of the seat, getting wetter. This way I could raise myself slightly off the stool so that my pubes were only just making contact. This was private pleasure. This was something I had done before. After all, you can do it whenever you want, yes? On a plane, on a bus, in a cab, in a restaurant, in the office, wherever there are people close enough to see if only they looked.

And usually no one can tell what I'm doing, which is half the fun, but when she pulled away, her lips wet with sucking, my nipple elongated and sore, the ice woman Delilah could perfectly well see my spread legs and the slow sliding of my fanny.

Her voice petered into a little gasp as she grabbed the seat of her own stool, and started to copy me, pushing her bottom hard back across the seat, and forwards again. The tiny muscles in my pussy were really convulsing now.

I held onto her thighs as she slid herself back and forth, and inched my fingers into her crack. Dampness started seeping through my knickers as the silk wrinkled away from my pussy. She bit her lip hard as she rubbed herself faster. I felt the cool leather meeting my sex lips and I nearly squealed out loud as they spread open, my little clit peeping out and retracting as it, too, made contact with the hard seat. Delilah could tell what was happening. I wanted her to see my knickers in the shadow of my skirt, and she was gyrating her hips under my hands, grinning at me, both of us in a private circle of excitement.

'Clara,' she hissed, her face suddenly close to mine. 'I need fucking!'

I didn't quite know what she meant. Did she mean me, or did she want to get one of the men in the bar? I wasn't having that.

'You're not going anywhere, lady.'

I pushed my fingers into her pussy and parted her, feeling the velvety smoothness of her sex lips as I opened them, ran my fingers up and down the crack and felt its soft wetness, the frills of her lips limp with desire. I'd never done this before. Ever. Not even close, yet now my forefinger was poking at this woman's cunt, and her cunt was sucking it in as if it was a little cock, and I wanted to do it. The stronger the pull from her cunt, the more I gasped, rubbing myself more frantically across the stool as droplets of desire stained the seat.

She closed her eyes. Her eyeballs rolled under her purplish lids, her eyelashes so long on her white cheeks. Somehow I'd had that effect on her, and I was in charge now. I took one of her hands, still holding my breast, and thrust it under my skirt. Her fingers were cool, and long, and I pulled them right into me, hooked my knickers aside, pushed her fingers inside so she could feel the strip of sticky hair and the cunt pulsing with desire beneath.

My mouth was against hers and, as her fingers mirrored what mine were doing, parting my sex and pushing inside, I kissed her, loving the soft give of her mouth, the grating of her teeth, my tongue pushing between those teeth to get at her, her tongue coming out at me, filling my mouth, making me want to suck on it.

My finger was up inside her now, pushing hard, feeling her body closing tight, and her fingers were parting me, stirring up delicious tremors of excitement. We kissed frantically, our mouths hard on each other, our hands pushing and pulling at each other, my leg curling up around hers, our bar stools right up close, rocking with our motion, and I realised that any minute we were going to fall right off onto the wooden floor, puncture the moment, lose it, lose everything.

'What shall we do? I've got to do this!' I hissed into her mouth. 'Where can we go?'

She pulled away, glanced over my shoulder at whoever was still in the bar.

'We stay right here. No one here. No one cares.' She smiled, her eyes half closed. She was like a Siamese cat. 'Free to do whatever we want. So show me what you're going to do to me, honey.'

So still kissing her, still keeping her impaled on my fingers, I dragged my Delilah off her stool and guided her sideways to the nearest Chesterfield sofa and as we tottered across the floor I was deliciously aware of my knickers reduced to a wet twist stuck unevenly up my crack, dark and soaking with my juices.

We tumbled onto the sofa, and oh God now she was on top of me, her light weight pinning me down, knocking the breath out of me, and our slim female legs and arms twined around each other. We had left our leather stools behind us, wet with our excitement, and our pussies were grinding up against each other, my thighs hooked around her hips, her pussy pushing and shoving, mine bucking against hers, her fingers peeling my knickers off, opening my throbbing cunt, our fingers finding their ways back in, our mouths kissing, sucking, pushing, so sweet.

As my cunt welcomed her fingers right inside me I flung my head back for a moment and glimpsed the room around us. We weren't alone. We knew that already, but now the barman and his cougars and some other people seemed to be jostling in the corner of my eye, I couldn't tell how close, watching us, I thought, but not crowding us, but that just made my cunt clench with more filthiness. My sore nipples brushed against my new lover's prickly sequinned dress, my breasts squashed up against her, her skirt round her waist, her bottom up in the air, held up by my fingers.

The fire spat and crackled near my cheeks. Feet stepped across the wooden floors, thudded across the rugs. Voices whispered and laughed. A siren called far down in the city. And Delilah's finger brushed over my clitoris, making me jerk up at her.

Delilah's cheeks were suffused with a hectic flush as I slammed my fingers into her again and she started to come, pulled back as if sucked by a tide and then throwing herself over me, her mouth grabbing mine, her fingers fucking me like crazy.

I watched her bucking back and forth across me, her mouth open now and her eyes blue and unblinking, fixed on mine. Her face was eerily calm, but there were high, keening cries coming from her as I pumped at her, and I was so aroused by watching what I'd done to her, the wild pleasure that was overwhelming her, that my own pleasure began to ebb slightly, and she knew it because she started to lick at me again, my mouth, pushing it open, panting her breath into me, pushing her finger into me, pushing up past my clitoris, pulling it out again, leaving spirals of hot desire, circling her finger just there, teasing me, then at last pushing in and remorselessly staying there.

'Gotta keep up!' she gasped as we rocked each other.

And so the wildness coiled through me, jagged and sharp. I heard myself crying out like she had done, my hands scrabbling to keep a hold of her as she screamed again, and at last I came, gripping her fucking fingers and shuddering with total abandon.

We slumped on top of each other as our climaxes faded. I was spread out under her, helpless as a colt, a trickle of pussy juice sliding down my inner thigh.

At last she slid off me, light as a feather, and stood up. I lay on the sofa, the fire crackling beside me, staring up at her long, white legs walking away from me, the shadow under her tight dress, that warm wet place where I had just been.

She stepped over to the bar and murmured to someone. I sat up shakily, yanking my skirt back over my legs, failing to find my lost knickers.

'Maybe I should go,' I stammered. She seemed to be ignoring me now. I scrabbled for my shoes. I thought I'd better make my exit, before I was thrown out.

She put her hand out to stop me as I passed.

31

'We could have another drink. We could go out on the town,' she suggested, handing me another daiquiri. 'Or we could just go straight down to your room?'

'How do you know I'm staying here?'

'I own the place.' She smiled, and chinked my glass. 'So I know everything about you.'

Drama Queen
Heather Towne

'I-I only got him six weeks ago,' Makayla snuffled, her lower lip trembling. 'B-but we'd made a real connection, you know?'

Kim put an arm around the girl's quivering shoulders, said, 'I know. I'm sooo sorry.'

The two young women stared at the goldfish floating belly up in the goldfish bowl.

'Nemo was a good fish,' Kim commented softly, sliding her left hand down over Makayla's hand, squeezing it.

'Th-the best!' Makayla burst into tears.

Kim hugged the girl tighter. 'Hey, don't cry. He's gone to a better place.' She brought the girl's hand up and kissed it, lightly tongued it. 'But I'm here for you. I'll always be here for you. I'm not going anywhere.'

The tall, willow-thin redhead turned Makayla around in her arms. She gazed lovingly, lustfully at her sobbing friend, then lifted the girl's chin with her fingers, brushed some of the tears off Makayla's chubby chocolate cheeks.

Makayla blinked her large liquid-brown eyes, her voluptuous body shuddering with a brave gulp. 'Th-thanks, Kim. You're the best – too.'

Kim smiled, her green eyes shining, feeling the heat of her friend's lush body so close, the hot, panting breath of the girl. She traced her wet fingertips over Makayla's cheeks, down to the young woman's lips, ran them along the soft plush pair. Then she moved her head closer and gently pressed her own glossy red lips to Makayla's cheek, kissing, licking away the young woman's tears.

Makayla shivered, not sure what was happening. She'd only known Kim for a couple of months, since they'd met at the sandwich shop. They'd struck up an instant rapport, Kim, being a year older, exhibiting patience and understanding of Makayla's relative immaturity as befitted her experience.

'Um, well, I guess I'll get over it,' the unabashed drama queen admitted, sniffling.

'I know you will,' Kim murmured, brushing her moist lips over Makayla's lips. 'But will I get over you, girl?' She pulled Makayla even closer, so that their hot bodies pressed together, beat together. She firmly planted her mouth on Makayla's mouth.

Makayla's eyes went wide, wide and dry. Her friend's lips were moving against her lips, the girl's arms sliding down her curved back and onto her mounded bum cheeks.

She'd never been consoled like this before. Most of her friends and family just barely tolerated her emotional outbursts, had learned to ignore them. But Kim was different – way different – so sensitive and caring, attuned to Makayla's feelings and needs. Still, the pretty redhead's hands digging into Makayla's bum cheeks, her tongue searching for an opening between Makayla's lips, was a little over the top for such a solemn occasion.

Makayla jerked her head back. 'Um, I guess I'd better bury Nemo. A private ceremony, I think, would be best.'

Kim licked her lips, tasting Makayla's blueberry lipgloss, breathing deep of the girl's peachy body spray. 'Are you sure? I'm here for you, Makayla. Whenever you need me. However you need me.'

'Yeah, I'm good,' Makayla gulped.

Kim brought over a new goldfish the next day, a black moor, Nemo the Sixth. Now that she'd baited the hook, she knew there would be other overemotional occasions to reel the cute girl in.

* * *

Two nights later, Kim received a frantic phone call.

'It's me, Kim! Makayla! I'm stuck! My stupid car broke down! I'm scared! I don't know –'

'Where are you?' Kim responded, quickly plunging her free hand into her panties, over the top of her tingling pussy.

She was sprawled out on her bed at home, in just her bra and panties. She'd been waiting hopefully for just such a call from her close friend. And now the sound of Makayla's sweet, shrill voice, the girl's heavy, panicked breathing, sent currents of sexual electricity coursing through her lean body, charging her pussy. She slid her fingers through her trim ginger fur, over her slick, puffy pink lips. 'Talk to me, girl!' she exhaled.

'Well, um, I was driving home from the sandwich shop, right?' Makayla took a deep breath that swelled her swollen chest, Kim's swollen pussy lips. 'And, all of a sudden-like, my car just died! And-and I can't get it started!'

Kim pulled the cellphone out of her ear and punched the speaker button, popped up a picture of Makayla's smiling face on the display, and then pushed her bra up over her breasts. She propped the small handheld up on her emptied bra and cupped a taut, creamy-white cone of heated flesh beneath, rubbing her pussy with her other hand, staring at Makayla's gorgeous, grinning face urging her on, like the girl's breathless voice vibrating through her body.

'Um, you still there, Kim?'

Kim moaned, squeezing her tit, buffing her clit. 'I'm here for you, sweetheart! Always!' She pinched her stiffened nipple, and her body arched, clit throbbing under her rubbing fingertips. 'But, uh, where exactly are you?' she groaned.

Makayla looked out the windshield at the darkened street. She had to drive through an industrial section of town to get home, and now the long, deserted warehouses and looming, empty factory buildings frightened her in the dark. There was no one around – no one to help her if someone happened along and found her trapped in her dead car. The night was hot, but she had all the windows rolled up, the doors locked.

'Um, I'm not sure. I'm no good with directions. You know the route I take. You drove me home once, remember?' Her voice trilled on the thin edge of self-induced hysteria. 'I'm in the middle of all these big plants and warehouses and stuff! All by myself!'

Kim bit her lip, Makayla's desperate voice making her desperate. Her hand bulged her cotton panties, flying back and forth, other hand kneading her uncupped breasts, fingers pulling on the pulsating cherry-red tips. Makayla's face bounced right before her. 'I know where you are, sweetie!' she gasped. 'I'm coming for you, baby! I'm coming –'

Makayla's ear rang with Kim's muffled shriek.

Kim shuddered, jumped, riding her clit-polishing fingers, her nipple-pinching digits, Makayla's face and voice, to the dizzying heights of phone-sex ecstasy.

'You're going to come and get me?' Makayla innocently asked.

'Yes! God, yes!'

Kim easily located Makayla's late-model purple Chevy Sprint parked next to the curb on Industrial Boulevard. She drove past the disabled vehicle and then made a U-turn, pulled up behind.

Makayla jumped when Kim tapped on the window, then, when she recognised her friend, dropped the tyre iron she'd been gripping. She rolled the window down an inch with shaking fingers.

'It's me – Kim,' Kim explained. The warm gush of air from Makayla's heavy sigh flooded her face, and her pussy tingled anew. She'd put on a pair of white short-shorts and a green halter top, and her long smooth limbs shone porcelain under the streetlight, her freshly painted lips glistening in a reassuring smile.

Makayla was still dressed in her sandwich-shop uniform, the tight tan blouse barely holding back her full breasts, tight black stretchpants moulding to the generous curves of her hips and butt. The girl's ebony skin gleamed dark and velvety, like her eyes.

Kim helped Makayla step out of the car, then hugged the young woman. Makayla shivered, despite the heat of the night. Kim reluctantly let go of the girl and looked inside the vehicle. 'You ran out of gas,' she announced, bobbing her head back out and up. 'That's all.'

'B-but I just filled up the tank a couple of days ago,' Makayla stammered. 'At least, I think I did.'

Kim squeezed the girl's bare arm, briefly caressed the satiny flesh. 'No worries. I'll drive you to a gas station, we'll get some gas and come back and get your car started.'

Makayla smiled wide with relief. She allowed Kim to take her hand and lead her back to Kim's orange Firefly. Kim opened the passenger-side door for the girl, watching Makayla's plump buttocks clench and ripple as she climbed into the seat.

'You all right now?' Kim asked, sliding into the driver's seat close to Makayla.

Makayla's teeth shone white, her shoulders heaving in a sigh, her big breasts along for the ride, stretching her top. 'Yup. Thanks so much, Kim! I really appreciate it!'

Kim grinned. She held out her arms, and Makayla filled them with her ripe young body.

'That's what good friends do for each other,' Kim whispered in the girl's ear. 'Among other things.' She kissed Makayla's neck, pressing her lips against the warm, sensitive skin.

Makayla pulled her head back when she felt Kim's moist tongue-tip touch her neck. She stared into Kim's shining eyes, goose bumps prickling her arms.

Kim moved her head forward, pressed her lips into Makayla's, holding the girl so tight that their breasts mashed together, Makayla's large soft ones smothering Kim's smaller, firmer ones. She used the hot, tight confines of the car, Makayla's rescued gratitude, to slide her tongue in between Makayla's parted lips and bump it up against the girl's tongue.

Makayla jerked, surprised, shocked – excited. Her friend really did like her, a lot! So what was wrong in showing it? She owed Kim, for helping her deal with the loss of her fish and the breakdown of her car. She lifted her tongue to Kim's gently probing tongue, and the two young women swirled their lickers together.

The slippery pink appendages wrapped around one another, more urgently, more openly, more erotically. Kim surged with delight. She slid her hands off Makayla's back and brought them around, in between, onto the girl's overblown breasts. She squeezed the heavy pair, kneaded the thick, heated flesh.

Makayla shuddered, her friend's hands on her sensitive breasts, the girl's fingers on her electric nipples, flooding her body and brain full of feeling. She couldn't think straight, couldn't resist what was happening to her – another woman frenching her, fondling her breasts and nipples. Her pussy brimmed with wicked wet sensation.

Kim yanked Makayla's blouse out of the girl's pants and shot her hands up and under, clasping Makayla's bare breasts. They filled her slender hands to overflowing, hot and ripe and smooth. Makayla moaned, and Kim broke away from the girl's stiffened tongue and dropped her head down to suck on Makayla's tits.

Makayla pushed Kim back, fumbled her blouse back down and turned around in the seat, suddenly coming to her senses. 'Let's get that gas, huh?' she gasped.

Kim sat stunned for a moment, her mouth open and tongue hanging out, awfully empty hands grasping at thin air. Then she gave her head a shake and rasped, 'Oh, sure. OK.' Disappointed now, but confident that in the future she'd be driving Makayla to more than just a fuel station – driving the luscious chocolate bunny wild.

* * *

'I-I wanted to surprise him, you know? S-so I snuck into his apartment with the key he gave me. He was supposed to be sleeping, because he works the graveyard shift.' Makayla's long, fluttering eyelashes flung tears, her voice rising to a wail. 'But … he was in his bedroom, all right! Having sex with another woman!'

She burst out crying again, and Kim tightened her grip on the girl's sobbing shoulders. They were in Makayla's bedroom, sitting on Makayla's bed. Kim had rushed over as soon as she'd gotten the plaintive phone call, being there for her good friend.

'It wasn't even anybody I know!' Makayla cried through her hands. 'Just some – some slut!'

'You mean, a professional?' Kim breathed in apparent

amazement. She slid her right hand down off Makayla's shoulder to gently but firmly clutch the side of the girl's bulging breast.

Makayla jerked her head up and stared at Kim. 'Yeah! I think so! Judging from the leopard-print skirt and fishnet stockings and thigh-high leather boots and neon-red tube-top I saw lying around all over the floor.'

'The bastard!' Kim hissed.

'We'd been dating four months, you know? I thought maybe we had something, like, special.'

'Men!' Kim gritted.

'He tried to say that *she* came on to him, just showed up at his place out of the blue, that she meant nothing to him. But I was too upset to listen.'

'The cheating bastard!'

'Yeah!' Makayla's wet, angry eyes softened. 'You're the best, Kim. You came right over when I called you. You've never let me down.' She kissed her friend.

Kim thrilled at Makayla's spontaneous burst of feminine affection. 'Let's just put men – boys – out of our minds, shall we?' she said, wrapping her hand right around Makayla's breast and squeezing. 'It's just us girls now.' She kissed Makayla, hard, on the mouth.

Makayla turned on the bed to face Kim. She lifted her shaking hands, shot them into Kim's red tresses. She mashed her mouth against Kim's, anxiously kissing back, the pair's friendship flowering in a frenzy.

Kim jabbed both her hands in between their over-heating bodies and grabbed both of Makayla's breasts. She kneaded the well-formed mounds through the girl's thin top, fingers finding and pinching thickened nipples, darting her tongue into Makayla's mouth – where Makayla welcomed it with hers.

They excitedly frenched, their breath coming in hot, humid gasps. Makayla's sparkly fingernails bit into Kim's scalp, Kim's hungry hands groping Makayla's breasts. Their tops popped off like they had no business ever being on, and they clasped their naked torsos together, heated flesh and rigid tips of their boobs meeting and melding in the most delicious manner.

Their flailing pink tongues now spoke a common language of lesbian eroticism, their breasts and bodies surging together to complement their mutual lust. Kim pushed Makayla back onto the girl's bed and climbed over on top of her, clutched the young woman's dark breasts and painted the darker tips with her tongue in swirls.

'Ohmigod! Yes, Kim! Suck my titties!' Makayla squealed, throwing up her arms, thrusting out her chest.

The impassioned words were music to Kim's burning ears, a siren song. She pushed Makayla's heavy breasts together and swiped her tongue back and forth over the fat nipples. Then she sucked one up into her mouth, tugged on it with her lips, cheeks billowing; then did the same to the moaning girl's other edible nipple.

Makayla's buds blossomed still more, stiffening even harder, swollen huge and throbbing thanks to Kim's luscious sucking. The girl's chest burned, her body shimmering, Makayla feeling the heavy tug of Kim's lips on her tits all through her.

Most boys just proffered a few perfunctory sucks, hurting her boobs with their rough, hurried groping, before stuffing their cocks into her pussy. But Kim really knew what she was doing, really paid patient attention to the pressure points of delight on Makayla's breasts, one woman to another.

Kim pulled Makayla's left nipple back taut with her lips, then released it, letting it pop back; then did the same to Makayla's other fully engorged nipple. Making the girl jump with wicked joy at each heady snap-back.

Then Kim piled Makayla's breasts up even higher, the thick flesh billowing out between her fingers, and she bit into one of Makayla's glistening up-thrust nipples.

'Oooh!' Makayla squealed, the pain and pure pleasure zapping her being, her pussy full of feeling. Kim bit into her other nipple, pulled it back with her teeth, and Makayla full-body shuddered, staring down at the grinning woman with the dark, pulsating nipple between her strong, white teeth.

Kim flogged Makayla's stretched nipples with her tongue again, twirled it all around the gasping girl's areolas. They were as wide as coasters, a deeper dark than the rest of her delicious breast-flesh, pebbled throughout their awesome circumferences. Kim tongued every sensitised inch of them, hot and wet and slurping, setting Makayla's breasts and body wildly trembling.

Finally, she looked up over Makayla's bathed and heaving tits and asked, 'Would you like to suck on my boobs?'

Makayla's wide eyes blinked. 'I-I'd love to!' the girl enthused. How could she refuse?

Kim crawled up higher on Makayla's laid-out body, planted her hands on either side of the girl's head, sticking her chest into Makayla's shining face. Makayla gulped, brought her arms back down. Her dark hands slid onto Kim's ivory breasts, gripping the firm cones, and it was Kim's turn to moan with delight.

Makayla grinned, gazing up into Kim's fluttering eyes. She squeezed Kim's tits, making the woman shudder. Kim's breasts were warm and pliable, the flush nipples jutting. Makayla worked Kim's tits with her hands, revelling in the feel, the response she elicited from her girlfriend. And then she bobbed her head up and stuck out her brilliant pink tongue and flicked it against a straining nipple.

'Yes!' Kim cried, nipples seizing up even tighter, body surging with heat, as Makayla teased the other nipple with the firm, wet, flicking tip of her tongue, grasping Kim's breasts tight.

Makayla swelled with eroticism, and confidence. She pinched Kim's nipples up even longer, so that they stuck out obscenely. Then she slapped them with her tongue, swirled her lush licker all around their outthrust arousal, painting them with pleasure. Until she pulled her tongue back into her mouth, parted her lips wider, and sucked one of Kim's breast-tips right inside her mouth, nursed on it.

'Yes, Makayla! God, yes, girl, suck on my tits!' Kim gasped, her body and breasts burning, Makayla's tongue and lips setting her ablaze.

Makayla urgently tugged on Kim's one nipple, then spat the rubbery protuberance out and swallowed up Kim's other nipple, vacced it with a passion, taking to lesbian tit-sucking like a baby to its mother's breasts. All the while grasping and groping Kim's reddened boobs.

Until, at last, Kim pulled away, popping her gleaming nipples out of Makayla's greedy mouth, her bruised breasts out of Makayla's mauling hands. Staring into the girl's shining wide eyes, Kim crawled lower down Makayla's undulating body. She gripped the waistband of Makayla's purple booty shorts and pulled down.

The girl's pussy was shorn of pubes, dark lips puffed and glistening with moisture. Kim saw the fear, the fever in her friend's eyes, then felt Makayla's trembling hands on her head, pushing her down. She pressed her lips against Makayla's slit, shot her tongue into the pink.

'Oh, Jesus!' Makayla screamed, body and breasts jumping.

Kim grabbed up the girl's splayed tits and worked them with her hands, as she licked Makayla's pussy. It was wild, wanton, extreme. It wasn't anything Makayla's handful of boyfriends had ever done for her, and she stared down at Kim with dewy eyes, her lush body and cunt suffused with caressing fire.

Kim lapped up and down, tonguing Makayla's slit and clit over and over, stroking long and hard and wet. Getting wetted in return. The tangy taste of the girl was sublime, the heady scent dizzying. But this erotic activity was better shared – licking and getting licked. It was time to fully immerse Makayla in the wanton depths of lesbianism, turn her friend into her lover.

Kim rolled over onto her back, unfastened her shorts and slid them along her legs, kicked them away. Then she scrambled up on all fours on the bed, swung a leg over Makayla's body and positioned herself so that she was facing Makayla's pussy from the opposite angle, while her pussy was over Makayla's face – the girl–girl 69.

Kim grasped Makayla's full, quivering thighs and plunged her head down, her tongue into Makayla's pussy. She felt the girl instinctively thrust her mound upwards, so that Kim could burrow her tongue even deeper into the pink. The entire length of Kim's licker was quickly embedded in Makayla's tight, juicy, silken tunnel.

'Ohmi–! Jesus!' Makayla shrieked, her hot breath steaming against Kim's brimming pussy. She stared up into Kim's downy ginger fur, the puffed pink lips, shaking with emotion, feeling Kim's mouth-organ squirm around inside her overheated sexual core. It was amazing, sensational; better than any one-way cock could ever offer.

Kim breathed deep of Makayla's pussy, nose pressed to the girl's engorged lips, tongue writhing around inside the oven-hot, super-wet velvet tunnel. And then she shivered with delight, as she felt Makayla's hands grip her bum cheeks, felt Makayla's tongue touch her own sodden pussy. She grinned into Makayla's pussy, over-joyed and overcome at finally getting the girl to take the plunge.

Makayla tentatively licked at her girlfriend's slit, barely skimming the plumped lips with the tip of her tongue, riffling through the red fur. But then she heard and felt Kim's moan, deep inside her own body, Kim's pussy-buried tongue vibrating her pleasure out into Makayla. And, inspired, the girl sunk her fingernails into Kim's taut buttocks and her tongue into Kim's electrified pussy. Makayla plugged into Kim, like Kim was plugged into her, the women joined.

They filled each other with their tongues. Then fucked one another, pumping their bladed tongues back and forth in between pussy lips and deep into pink. Until

Kim found Makayla's swollen clit with her tongue, then her lips, sealing her mouth around the pulsating button and sucking. Makayla's muffled cry reverberated through both of them.

Makayla pulled her tongue out of Kim's pussy and back into her mouth. Her lips sought out, found, Kim's puffed-up pink button. She sucked on Kim's clit, her head dizzy and body fiery with the other woman sucking on her intimate source of ultimate pleasure.

The pair sucked, tongued, nipped one another's clits, oralising each other to the very edge of explosive orgasm. And when Kim felt a premature squirt, she backed off her slurping tongue and sucking lips. She rolled off Makayla, shaking off the girl's grasping hands and mouth. Then she elbowed up on the bed and scissored her ivory legs into Makayla's ebony limbs, squishing their pussies together.

Both women shrieked at the erotic impact.

They clutched each other's legs and pumped their pelvises, grinding their pussies together, glaring at one another. Makayla did it by instinct, Kim from experience.

The passion built to fever pitch, fed by the tingling memories of their mouths on each other's pussies, the wet-hot friction of their pussies now rubbing and rubbing together, merging as one ultra-erotic entity. They shuddered together against one another, squirting searing orgasmic juices, scorching ecstasy engulfing the pair and sending them sailing.

Afterwards, Kim held the glowing girl in her arms and reassured Makayla that the 'drama' would die down now that she'd be so close, now that they were 'real' girlfriends.

'You mean, now that you drove me into your arms by killing my goldfish, emptying my gas tank and setting my boyfriend up with a hooker?' Makayla responded. She grinned knowingly up at Kim, sticking out her tongue and teasing one of her lover's flared nipples.

Kim grinned back, sheepishly. She hugged Makayla tight. 'I didn't actually kill your goldfish. *That* just happened by chance.'

Letting Go
Lucy Lush

I used to breathe power. It was my very essence. There was no one I could not control or manipulate. Nature blessed me with the looks and the wits to stand my ground and stand above others. I worked hard to accrue my considerable wealth, asking for and giving no quarter along the way, gaining in confidence all the time, learning to take whatever I wanted. If I walked into a room it would be me all eyes were on, me that caused mouths to dry and juices to flow, that broke a hundred hearts when I selected my plaything for the evening from the array of hopefuls. And now in a flash it has gone. I have yielded everything to a girl, and I don't even know her name.

Until very recently I had all this. I hunted in the clubs whenever I wanted and always got my prey. You might wonder why the girls came there and let it happen, but I knew that they would, night after night, the challenge and their curiosity bringing them to my lair. Once I had chosen them, there was no escape. I used to be able to have any girl I wanted. You don't believe me? You would if you saw me and watched me at work, selecting my quarry and reeling them in. I ran on the basis that there was no one I could not catch if I set my mind to it. The bigger the potential challenge, the more I wanted to prove that I could succeed. My sexual CV looks like *the* most preposterous fantasising of a hormone-fuelled teenager, but it is all true.

Let me give an example. Just about a month ago I did something which for me was new: I seduced a mother and her step-daughter. One was white, one was black. Both were bold and brassy, both were jiggling and gibbering and threatening to self-combust if they didn't get up to some very dirty business now that they had a chance. However, for all their shared closeness and mutual desires there is no way they intended to end up naked together that night. Perhaps in a best-case scenario they hoped they might have been done in adjoining rooms, hearing each other's cries and competing to be the loudest. More likely they suspected they would get done up the same alley, or perhaps with one on the back seat of the car and one over the bonnet. I'm sure they suspected they would get one lover each, and even though they were where they were I bet neither in their wildest dreams thought that if they did end up sharing a lover it would turn out to be me.

The seduction nonetheless proved easy, because I worked out the psychology and played it just right. I liked the step-daughter more, with her pristine dark chocolate skin and her narrow, jutting bottom. However, I still went to the mother first and stood close, making her believe that *she* was my primary target, letting her know in very simple terms that I was going to fuck the arse off her. Whilst I boosted Mummy's ego and got her all hot and amenable, I let the stepdaughter's surprise and jealousy ferment for a while. It is simple human nature. No one likes to be second best, so take two people and fawn over one and the other will vie for your attention. They almost cannot help themselves. At the pivotal moment I drew the younger girl in too, so that they were side by side before me, looking up into my lustful eyes. To make up for my earlier inattention I kissed the girl first – soft and hot, with just enough passion for her to know I meant business. But as I did so, I ran my hand up the mother's thigh, right up beneath her too short skirt. I ignored her gasp and eased my hand between her legs, to cup and squeeze her warm, fleshy mound through the cotton of her dampening knickers.

I broke off while both were in the first burning rush of excitement. They were still breathless and mute as I switched my attentions, planting my lips instead on the woman's open, wet mouth. I ran my left hand up the girl's leg, under her even shorter skirt, gently prising her smooth thighs apart and cupping her smaller mound, feeling her heat through the lace beneath my fingers. They were hooked. All reason was lost to lust and alcohol, so I took their hands and led them away. I had already called my driver and she was waiting outside the club as instructed. I gave them champagne from the chiller cabinet and kissed them in turn as we were driven back to my apartment.

Once there I gave no time for circumspection or second thoughts. I had them bend over side by side and I stripped them of their knickers, displaying their open bottoms and puffy, desperate quims. I made them masturbate for me as I absorbed the sight and their differences, and got myself ready. Then I fucked them, going back and forth between them, using my brand-new, thickly veined, black strap-on dildo. When they were soaked, endlessly coming, and wholly under my spell, I even showed due deference and fucked Mummy up the bum, using a slightly smaller, smoother dildo from my collection. The younger girl had a very tight virgin bottom, but she ended up losing this precious cherry too, although even in her most furtive thoughts I doubt she would ever have dared deduce correctly who would be the one to take it from her (that was definitely one for *her* sexual CV – bum deflowered by her own father's wife!).

Seducing hetero girls in a gay club is easy. They go there because the atmosphere is less aggressive and the boys are there to have fun and dance and not bother the girls. Plus they like to see if they are attractive to other females, and think they can handle themselves if the inevitable happens and they get chatted up. It is safe and titillating, an exciting walk on the edge of a new world, which they can always pull away from if their courage falters – unless, of course, they run into me. But now for the first time in my life I can actually appreciate the massive thrill they feel when being swept away by the inexorable surge of a beautiful woman's attentions. For the first time in my life I have been seduced.

As I write this I have a decision to make. She has set out her terms and if I am to see her again, I must do so as her slave. I have already decided I must go to her. I have already chosen my shoes and clothes for the evening, trembling as I carefully selected a costume to attract yet show willingness to obey. I don't know what it was in her eyes, her kiss, or her electric touch that made me crumble so utterly in the first instance. But I did, and once she had shown me her secrets, I was totally lost to her. Although parts of me still show a vague effort to resist, I know that she already owns me, body and soul.

And so the last fuck I will have as a Goddess of Power was with that horny mother and her step-daughter. Perhaps that's why I'm clinging to the memory and feel a need to tell you about it. There were probably only ten years separating them and the mother obviously felt she was still too young for the good things in life to pass her by. The wedding ring had been removed and I guessed she saw the girl as more of a companion than someone supposed to be under her guardianship. They were at the club to 'wet the baby's head' – the child in question belonging to the daughter's best friend, a celebration to show that the tradition of unplanned teenage pregnancies amongst their circle was alive and well. At the time I made my move, so I learned, the best friend and her allies were crouched in the toilets bringing up way too many vodka shots.

Anyone who says that threesomes are overrated is a liar. How else are you going to get fucked in both holes at once? I had them buckle up and do it to me, right after I had finished pumping Mummy's backside. I straddled the girl and rode her, sliding my slick pussy up and down the thick dildo before bending forward to kiss her and have her hold my bottom apart. I had the lusty MILF do my arse – mainly because she looked like she had used a harness before, and my bum is still tight and requires tender handling. I directed their pace and controlled the rhythm so that I could feel the toys in sequence within me, almost touching as they went in and out of my leaching passages.

I love to be filled like this, especially when the girl beneath me is a young chocolate-skinned slut and the one behind me a big-titted bleached-blonde bitch with a fat enough rump to drive the dildo purposefully into mine. I had thought it was the best feeling a female could experience, but I was to be proved wrong. We played many dirty games that night, and I brought the woman and the girl closer together than they had ever been or even imagined. Then, when I was finally tired of coming, I sent them away. I went back to the club some two weeks later to see if they had returned to find me, hopeful of a repeat performance, but instead I saw HER, and from that instant my life changed beyond recognition.

She was standing in a darkened corner near the bar, sipping from a martini glass. There was a pretty, petite brunette at her side talking up at her, but she was ignoring the companion and staring fixedly at me. Her hair was a jet-black bob and her eyes were large and feline green. Her nose was small and slightly upturned, showing the slant of black nostrils against her snow-white skin. Her lips were burgundy red and shining, the bottom one a plump morsel of delectable flesh. I have never wanted to kiss someone so urgently in all my life.

Her breasts were dove-smooth and threatened to spill their ample weight from her leather corset, which came in sharply at the waist to accentuate her wide hips. She was beautiful, completely beguiling. I could feel the familiar tingle in my loins but it was accompanied by the alien sensation of my stomach flipping and dancing with butterflies. We stood, our gazes locked, almost a battle of wills to see who would crack and approach the other first. In the end, she raised her forefinger and curled it towards herself, three, maybe four times, giving me the sign to come to her. And I did.

What is seduction if not the striking of a deal between two or more parties? You each make your bargain and the one with the stronger will gets it on *their* terms, even if all stand to be satisfied with the outcome. It is about the power to make people do your bidding and be happy to pay the price. It is something I always succeed in, yet I lost this deal before we had even begun the negotiation process, before a word had even been said, and all it took was a kiss.

As I approached, her mouth broke into a half-smile of triumph but she didn't dwell on her victory. I stood before her and she held my gaze for just a few seconds, then her arm came out to encircle my waist and pull me in. The warm swell of her lips yielded as I sank into her and she let me enjoy their exquisite fullness before her tongue pushed my lips apart and swirled around mine. My insides were molten. It felt like all my blood was surging in a tingling rush to the very centre of my sex. Her mouth was soft and warm, her movements exactly choreographed with mine. She let me suck her gorgeous bottom lip and then she gently caught mine between her perfect teeth.

She pulled away and held my gaze again, still

half-smiling at my breathlessness. I wanted to be assertive but my strength had flown. My legs had turned to jelly and my tongue was immobile, yearning not to speak but to be entwined once more with hers.

'Take me to your place,' she said. 'I'm going to fuck you.'

She teased me with her fingers in the back seat of my car, but wouldn't let me come. She made me walk into the apartment block reception and past the late-night concierge with my skirt pulled up and my bottom barely covered by my tiny panties. Although there are cameras in the lift, she hauled out her luscious tits and made me suck her gloriously swollen nipples. In my room we stripped quickly and for a while we made love like equals, a new experience for me. Soon though, when she was sure that I was defeated, she began to take control.

She sat on my face and smothered me in her soft, delicious bum. She ground her hips back and forth and covered my nose and mouth and cheeks in her flowing wetness. Then she told me to lick her, first her fragrant pussy, then her little bitter-sweet anus. I'm a dirty bitch, but that was the first time I had ever tasted another girl's behind. She had me stick my tongue right up her, licking and probing until the tight muscles relented and allowed me inside. As I carried out her orders, she leant forward and lightly and intermittently spanked the fat flesh of my shaven cunt.

She swivelled around and made me attend to her engorged clit, a neat button in shiny red peeping out of its protective surrounds. She pulled at her own nipples, stretching them to hard points as I lapped and sucked. I was elated when I made her come, hard and loud. I loved the way she wriggled and rode my face and covered me in her slick juices. It felt dirty and exhilarating to be used in such a manner by one so flawless, to be allowed to receive such a gift. She must have seen my eyes bright with adoration as she licked her cream from my glistening cheeks.

She told me I must trust her and I said I did. She told me that if I promised to put myself in her hands and obey her instructions, then she would give me the greatest pleasure of my life. I wanted to tell her that I loved her, but I remembered how often I had heard those words rush from the mouths of my chosen playthings, and how pitiful they always sounded. She crossed to my wardrobe and found silk scarves to bind my wrists to the bed. I have never once been tied before. She could see my panic rise and my resolve weaken, but she whispered in my ear and kissed me again to calm me.

I was hers now to do as she wanted. I had submitted my body and it was fizzing with the same trepidation and yearning anticipation that I had given to so many others. She kissed me all over, gentle touches and wet sucks from her enchanting lips. She spent ages at my nipples, making sure they were long and throbbing and dowsed in slimy saliva. Her bites there grew harder as she progressed but I never felt under threat. I was washed through with calmness despite my vulnerability. She teased the skin at my belly and made the muscles below ripple uncontrollably. Then she was down between my thighs and I was opening my legs wide for her, dying to receive whatever she would give me.

She rubbed the skin above my hood and then encircled my folds with her mouth and drew in her breath, shooting a mini gust of cold air over my hot, spit-wet clitty. She lapped and teased, but still would not make me come. Her fingers drifted up over my smooth mound and rested just above it on the flat of my tummy. She applied gentle pressure, just enough to make me feel an awakening tingle in my bladder. Then she slid her middle finger into my waiting pussy, curling it inside me and bumping it against the sweet-spot at the front, making me buck upwards from the mattress and cry out.

I had been touched there before. A few of my girls had found that place, but it had always seemed like a haphazard quest. Even my own private searches had proved it to be random and elusive. But this girl found it immediately, caressing the spongy pad and sending pulses of joy through my core. As she stroked me there, I felt the pressure increase on my belly until she was pressing at my bladder enough to make me squirm and panic.

I began to sob and plead, wanting her to continue her work inside me but scared of my lack of control and the imminent release.

'Be calm,' she whispered. 'All you have to do is let yourself go. Trust me.'

I was fretting and bucking but hurtling towards my orgasm. Her finger worked fast inside me and she lapped at my clit again and took me closer. For one fleeting moment I thought I was going to make it but then her pressure became too great and my bladder felt hot and expansive, and I was hit by an urgent need to urinate. I held my breath and tried to tense myself against it but she was down on my clit again, trying to counter my evasive actions. I pulled at the wrist ties to no avail. The feeling in my bladder grew and grew until it felt like it was burning inside me.

'I need to pee! I need to pee!' I cried.

'Do it!' she called out. 'Push now – let yourself go!'

Then it happened. Just as my urgency grew unbearable, I relented and unclenched my muscles and as I did so the ache melted into the boiling surge of my rising climax as it took over and burst from me. It was so intense I screamed. The release was incredible and unconfined. I managed to keep my eyes open and saw my gush splash up her arm as she wanked the orgasm from me. I remember her smiling down at my awestruck expression as she sucked her finger and palm clean. I was panting for air and unable to speak, my whole body still trembling and alive. She gave me only a minute or so to recover, and then I felt her finger inside me again, finding my most sensitive spot at once.

She did me again, pressing once more on my belly and forcing me to feel the need to pee while she stroked inside my pussy. My climax had no time to recede and I felt it quickly building once more, along with an almost overwhelming urge for relief. This time I knew how to let myself go and as I felt the pussy and uterine contractions, I lifted my knees and thrust my hips upwards from the bed to give her greater access. She withdrew her finger at the last moment and I came massively, even stronger than the previous time if that were possible. I watched the stream of liquid squirt in a jet from inside me, some three feet into the air before it arced over me and splashed down onto my tits and chest, onto my neck and chin, even into my shocked, open mouth.

Afterwards I lay dazed and euphoric, revelling in the wetness on my body. It was not thin and watery, but slightly viscous and velvety, like a dilute cordial. It was not just piss, it was *come*. The feeling running through me was nothing short of sublime. I whispered that I wanted her to do it again even though I couldn't have taken another burst of bliss so soon. She just arched her eyebrows dismissively and stayed silent. Her sudden detachment burned because I was aching for her. I needed to have her close, to tell me that she would do it for me any time I asked. I didn't care what the cost was, I just prayed that I could give her something in return to keep her with me.

She was so utterly beautiful. For the first time I knew what it was to *need* someone, as so many needed me, how *wanting* was every bit as exhilarating as the power to cast someone away without a thought. Her beauty had filled me, coursing through my insides and swelling every cell until it was too much to take and her liquid grace had spurted from me. I was tripping over the poetry I thought the moment needed, trying to explain how wonderful she made me feel, to give her some flowery words that might draw her in. I just sounded like a complete idiot and she regarded me coldly and talked over my silliness. She said that I would never see her again unless I agreed to do whatever she wanted to me. I nodded, dumbly. She scanned the surfaces and picked up my mobile phone from the cabinet. She then took a photo of my saturated cunt. She ascertained that the phone had my home number on it, and then she put it in her pocket.

She went to my robe again and pulled out a holdall and stuffed it with clothes she selected from my racks. She went around the room and studied my things, taking whatever interested her – some ornaments, my antique clock, a dildo or two, my underwear from the floor. She made a show of taking money from my purse, rolling it up and secreting it in her pussy. She knew I was powerless to stop her stealing from me, even without the restraints. Then she dressed, kissed me deeply, untied me and left.

Yes, I've tried to recreate what she did to me, but I cannot even get close. I sometimes find the spot but can't force the urge upon myself and have it break into that same unparalleled feeling of release. I cannot make myself squirt and so I have to let go of what I was and give myself over because nothing now is as important as being with her again. If I do not see her again or feel what she did to me then my life from now on will be pointless. Like some wretched drug addict I am utterly dependent and she is the heroine. I have been stripped of my assurance and potency and cannot function or concentrate. I stammer and stumble because my mind is always filled with her. Worst of all, I know I am in love.

She phoned me this week, late at night. She told me where I could meet her and that if I did I would come to her as her slave and from that point she would be free to do as she pleased with me. She gave me a long list of indignities I could be expected to perform as her possession. She might make me strip in front of strangers. She might have me masturbate in a crowded cinema, unseen by most, but all around would be able to smell my arousal. She would have some of her other slaves fuck my bum, one after another, but forbid me to touch myself and take my pleasure. She would spank and sometimes cane me. She might make me suck a man's huge cock, and have me pay him for it. Other things, I can't even tell you. She plans to transform me into her smitten whore, devoid of any purpose except to do her bidding.

I used to be Queen of All, but I am abdicating in favour of an existence of ignominy and degradation. I am about to lose all the comfort and control and security my life provided. I might give over every part of me and yet still be left with nothing. But I have to go to her. If you could feel what she made me feel, you would know that I have to go.

A Taste of London
Chrissie Bentley

'Breakfast, ma'am?'

I awoke with a start. Through the black fabric eye-mask I was wearing, I could tell that the cabin lights were still dimmed, but the in-flight movie was over and the rising hum of voices told me that my fellow passengers were beginning to stir. We must be close to landing.

I opened my mouth to speak, and instead felt something fat and fleshy brush my lips with wiry fur, then spread to draw my face into its depths. A hand on the back of my head, guiding my movements while I collected my thoughts, and the thick, honeyed wetness of a well-oiled cunt shaped itself around my tongue as it swirled and twisted through those dark, magical depths.

I reached up, and grasped warm skin and coarse hair and smooth belly; I stretched and felt breasts, taut against my palm as the nipples bored into my flesh. I squeezed as I sucked at the warmth on my face, drawing the folds into my mouth as my tongue burrowed deeper and my visitor leaned forward, forcing me back against the headrest of my seat. 'My God,' I thought. 'If this is how they treat you in Business Class, imagine what happens in First!'

'Ma'am? Breakfast?' The voice again, more insistent this time.

My brain jarred back to reality. I pulled off the eye-mask and saw the stewardess standing beside me, a silver tray in one hand, a coffee pot in the other. Her blue airline skirt was demurely buttoned and unruffled, her breasts simple shadows against her dark jacket and starched white blouse. Her smile was bright but it was also mechanical, exactly as you'd expect it to be if the highlight of your morning was the chance to serve breakfast to the red-eye brigade.

'Sorry. Thanks.' I took the tray and leaned back in my seat, smiled as she poured my coffee and watched her move on to the next aisle. Dreams like that I can do without. At least until I'm awake enough to enjoy them.

I have to confess, when my boss announced that he was sending me to England, it was difficult not to suppress a yelp of delight. I majored in English (and I mean English, no American authors) Lit at college, I'd been working in the New York office of a London company for almost five years – and I'd never once crossed the Atlantic. Now he was offering me a week there, and all I had to do was agree to attend (deep breath) a trade fair, two sales conferences and a couple of still unscheduled planning meetings. The rest of my time just that. My time. And so, ten days later ...

We landed, passed through the queues of lurking officialdom, and the unending lines at immigration where your reward for standing for an impatient hour was a smudged stamp on your passport and a deeply insincere 'Welcome to the United Kingdom' from the bored man at the desk. Then it was out onto the concourse where I scoured the crowd for my ride, the chauffeur who'd be waiting with my name on a handwritten placard.

'Bentley.'

Ah, there he ... oh, she ... is. I stepped forward. 'Hi, Chrissie Bentley.'

The short, plump-but-pretty girl smiled. 'Melissa Bishop.' Then, when she saw my look of surprise, 'It's OK, I've not been demoted. I just thought you could do with a friendly voice after your flight.' Melissa was my opposite number in the London office, the one I dealt with more often than not, and she was organising our booth at the trade fair. 'Plus, all our other drivers are booked up.' She nodded to a tall guy in full uniform, shepherding a party of Japanese towards the escalators. 'We've got people coming in from all over the world.'

'Damn, and I thought I was special,' I said with a pout.

'Well, you're the only American woman on the roster,' she replied. 'That should count for something,' and I knew exactly what she meant when we arrived at my hotel. The lobby was packed, wall-to-wall suits spilling out of the bar and restaurant area, with maybe twenty pairs of eyes swivelling to fix on us as we trailed the bellhop to the reception desk. I checked in and heard a voice behind me: 'Told you so, that's the Yank chick. A bit of all right, isn't she?'

I turned. A small knot of middle-aged salesmen raised their glasses to me, already drunk and reverting to type. A few years back, these exact same men would have been touring the country in a battered automobile, selling the latest craze in kitchen appliances out of a tatty old suitcase. Travelling salesmen. And then along came the 2000s, the Internet and globalisation, and now they were all Mobile Retail Representatives or some such nonsense. But they remained a bunch of unctuous creeps.

Melissa faded into the crowd with a cheery wave, and I turned towards the elevator. My room was on the fifteenth floor, gazing out across a cityscape that might once have taken my breath away. Now it just made me sad. Crane your neck out the window to the left, and the dome of St Paul's was peeping around a skyscraper, while an eyesore called the Pickle hung like a gleaming turd in the background. Strain to the right, and Westminster Abbey (I think) rose up among the office blocks.

Watch enough old movies on cable TV, and you could go through life believing that London is a forest of living history, church spires and turrets pointing skywards all over, as familiar to the modern viewer as it was to Dickens a century and a half ago, or Christopher Wren before him. But, framed by the window of my hotel, it could have been any city in the United States. I hoped it might look better from street level.

I unpacked, then stepped into the shower. No, I thought, I'll have a bath instead. I filled the tub, sank down into the water, and felt the stench of the flight finally float from my pores. I reached for my book, and a phone rang in my ear. There was an extension on the wall right above me. Wow, these Brits must enjoy their bath-time!

'Hello?'

'Chrissie, it's Melissa. I'm on my way up with some papers I need you to look over. Just wanted to make sure you weren't sleeping.'

'Actually, I'm ...' I paused. Oh, shit. It is a workday. 'Just give me five minutes, I'm in the tub.'

'That's OK, just wrap up in a towel or something. I'll only be a few minutes and you can jump straight back in.' She hung up, I dried off, and, taking her advice, I cocooned myself in the massive fluffy robe that was hanging on the back of the door. Moments later, Melissa tapped on my door.

'Sorry, I would have waited, but we have to get all our delegates' signatures into security before two. And, I thought, while I was here, we could have a quick look at these.' She handed me a few papers outlining the first of the projects that we'd be discussing this week. I reached for them and my robe tipped open, spilling one breast into view.

Melissa laughed. 'Oops. Happens to me all the time.' She laid a hand on her own –compared to mine – vast bosom. 'With calamitous results.' She twisted her torso from side to side and, even fully clothed and anchored by her bra, her breasts swung with a mind of their own.

I laughed, even as I felt a pang of envy. I was well aware from other friends just what a burden big breasts can be; and, besides, I'm quite content with my own slightly-more-than-a-handfuls. But there have been times when I wished that nature had been a little more generous – and now was not the time to be thinking about that. I tucked my escapee back under cover, knotted the cord a little bit tighter and sat carefully down on the bed, making sure that I didn't give Melissa another unexpected show. Although something in the way she looked at me – or, rather, the way she rather shyly didn't look at me – suggested that she wouldn't object if I did.

Melissa was right; the papers only took a few minutes to go through. She rose to leave, and then stopped. 'Dinner tonight? Do you have plans?'

'Nothing yet. To be honest, you're the only person I know in this entire country.'

She laughed, white teeth flashing around a glimpse of the tip of her tongue. 'I wasn't sure if you maybe wanted to mingle with the others this evening? Or if you want to meet up later and get away from the crowd?'

'I don't think I'm ready for the full weight of humanity.' I smiled, inwardly shuddering as I thought about the salesmen down in the lobby. 'Whatever you have planned sounds great.' We arranged for her to meet me in the lobby at seven, and I returned to my tub.

She was on time, and she was dressed to kill. But to kill whom? Plump she may have been, but Melissa carried her weight with a style and confidence that a lot of other women could learn from, choosing clothes that accentuated the colour of her eyes (green), the shade of her hair (blonde) and a body that a less weight-obsessed era would have described as curved in all the right places. All of them. I felt like a stick alongside her, and a not particularly well-dressed one. I wished I'd thought to pack some clothes that weren't either super-businesslike or ultra-comfortable. Of course I planned on shopping for some inbetweenies before the week was up, but it would have been smart to get a head start on the process.

Never mind. We caught a cab, ate Italian, then moved on to a nearby pub, busy enough that we weren't the sole focus of attention for all the men who lined the bar and the tables, but quiet enough that a handful, at least, spent most of the evening staring at us.

'Hey luv, you American?' A spotty youth swaggered over to our table, while three of his mates watched open-mouthed from the bar, all of them struggling to suppress their laughter.

I nodded.

'You look like someone I know. Do you have any English in you?'

'No.'

'Well, would you like some ...' and he lost the rest of his punchline in a snorting laugh, blushed bright red, then retreated to his choking chums. Melissa smiled sympathetically.

'You're going to get that a lot over the next few days, I think,' she warned me. 'But it was funny the first time I heard it. On a Thin Lizzy record – except it was Irish, then.'

We finished our drinks and walked out onto the street, looking around for a cab. 'I can have him drop you at your hotel, then carry on to my place,' Melissa explained.

'Unless you want to hit the hotel bar with me?' I suggested. 'I think it's open till late and, if it's not, there's always room service.' Looking back, it really does sound like I was making a pass at her, but I wasn't. Well, not completely, anyway. Rather, I didn't feel like sleeping yet, and I certainly wasn't ready to brave the salesmen alone.

She agreed, and maybe it was all in my mind again, but I think she eyed me oddly once more.

The bar was packed, and the desk clerk told us there was a half-hour delay in room service. 'It's a busy night,' he said, smiling apologetically. No problem; grabbing my arm, Melissa threaded us through the crowd, out onto the street again, and then down the road to a late-night convenience store, to stock up on some bottles of wine and snacks. 'This should keep us going for a while.' Then it was back upstairs, a grand uncorking and, after half an hour or so of chatter, 'So, is there a Mr Chrissie Bentley anywhere on the horizon?'

'Oh, I expect so.' I chose my words carefully. 'But so many of my friends, people I was at school and college with, are already divorced, separated or miserable that I really don't see the hurry.'

Melissa nodded. 'My mother once told me – and I was really rather shocked when she said it, because you don't want to think of your mother ... never mind. Anyway, she said you're not looking for someone you want to spend the rest of your life with. You need someone you want to spend the rest of your life having sex with. Because it doesn't matter what else you have going for you, that's the glue that holds a relationship together.'

'You have a wise mother,' I told her.

'Not really.' Melissa laughed. 'She's on to her third husband already. But the theory is sound. Plus, you can

75

have a lot of fun looking.' Her bright, questioning eyes seemed to seek out mine, and I felt myself flush. She saw it, too. 'So, no boyfriend?' she asked.

'No.'

'Girlfriend?'

'No.'

'Never? Or just not at the moment?'

Ah. I wasn't sure how to respond to that one, or whether I even wanted to answer honestly. 'Never' had a finality to it that might easily force her to change the subject, which was the last thing I wanted to happen. But 'not at the moment' suggested a depth of experience that might lead her equally astray. And while I pondered over my answer, she smiled as though she had picked up my uncertainty without me uttering a sound. 'It's all right, you don't have to answer if you don't want to.'

I reached out a hand and touched hers. 'It's not that I don't want to, I'm just not sure what the answer is.' In my entire life, I could count on two fingers the number of women I've 'been with' and, on both occasions, there was someone else in the room with us.

'Wow, you've had a threesome?' Melissa actually sounded rather impressed, even after I detailed the extent of my experiences, once with a friend where it didn't really get started, and once with a pair of handcuffs. Still Melissa chuckled. 'Doesn't sound so bad to me. The best I can manage is, a girlfriend and I played Blind Man occasionally – you know, where someone blindfolds you, then touches you in different places, and you can only wonder what they're touching you with?'

'Sounds fun.' I smiled, remembering playing much the same game with an old college boyfriend.

'Oh, it is,' she agreed and I saw her eyes flicker round the room, as though seeking out a scarf or something. I thought of the dream I'd had on the plane, and rummaged in my purse for the airline eye-mask. 'Would this work?'

She smiled, and reached for me then, pulling me towards her and kissing me gently on the mouth. My arms went to her waist, and a hand touched bare skin as her blouse untucked and rode up a little, her soft, plentiful flesh yielding to my touch. Her tongue flickered into my mouth, met mine and tussled for a moment, as her hand fell onto my breast. 'Now,' she whispered. 'Put on the blindfold. And then, I don't want you to make any move, unless I ask you to.'

I did as she asked and, in darkness, I sat stock still, trembling as I felt her fingers unbutton my blouse, before reaching around to unclip my bra. She slipped it off me, then pushed me lightly backwards onto the bed, while one hand undid the button on my skirt. My tights and panties came down in one swish, and I lay naked.

For a moment, nothing happened. I could still feel her weight on the mattress beside me, and I imagined her looking my body up and down. Then there was a slight breeze and a tickling sensation on my breasts, a thousand breathy wisps that teased my skin with wicked insistence. I tried to squint under the blindfold, but saw nothing; only as the sensation grew heavier and thicker, and I arched into a warm, wet nuzzle on one of my nipples, did I realise that it was her long hair that I felt, deliberately danced across my flesh. I reached out a hand to touch her, but she firmly pressed it back down. 'I told you, no moving unless I ask you to.'

There was a rustling sound. She undressed quickly, and there was a thump as she settled back on the bed. I didn't need my eyes to know that she was straddling my body, although there was no skin contact whatsoever. I tried to visualise her nakedness, wondered where those massive breasts might be hanging in relation to mine, and whether her nipples would be sized accordingly. But the unmoving silence remained unbroken until something brushed my lip, a slow left-to-right motion that I chased with my tongue, but it was too fast for me. There was a pause, before it swept back in the other direction. Once, twice, three times, and then it halted, heavy on my bottom lip. I tipped out my tongue to touch ... her pinkie.

I kissed it before she withdrew again, then recommenced the slow, sensual sweeping, one, two, three, stop. Only this time, when I tasted it, it was not a finger. I opened my mouth and nuzzled a nipple for the moment before it moved gently out of reach; then waited for the motion to begin again.

There was a scent in my nostrils that I recognised immediately. I folded my mouth over the light touch on my lip, a finger again, and tasted a teasing drip of pussy. I raised my head a little, sucked and the digit slid in to the first knuckle, as her other hand fell between my legs, teasing my outer lips, oiling itself on the juice that was flooding me.

The hand departed. I heard a slight slurp, and imagined Melissa licking me off her fingers. Then the weight around me lifted and shuddered, as she inched her body up mine, still not actually touching me, but sufficiently close that I could feel the warmth of her sex as it trekked up my belly, across one breast.

She wriggled a little, lowering herself so that my nut-hard nipple grazed her sex, and then lower still. The sensation was incredible. I had to ask her afterwards exactly what she was doing, then demanded a demonstration that I could actually watch as she spread her lips wide with her fingers, as wide as she possibly could, then placed her gaping snatch over my breast, until her clitoris collided with my nipple, the two super-sensitive nubs rubbing together for a few exquisite moments. That was what I felt in the darkness, that was what I was still feeling as her loins continued their upward journey and, when they reached their next destination, I had no need at all to ask what she'd done.

I lost myself in her flavour and scent, my tongue

darting, drilling, dancing across her hot wetness until, with her hands in my hair, tugging and twirling, my blindfold flew off and my eyes, too, could feast upon the vision that hung above me: the thick crotch beneath the expansive belly that ground itself into my mouth, and the pendulous breasts that brushed my forehead, with nipples that looked like Hershey's Kisses. Melissa was still crying the last of her orgasm as I pulled her down, and her breast to my mouth. I began suckling her and, when she came again, my hand buried deep inside her, her breast filling my mouth, I felt my own massive orgasm building up within me.

So did she. Melissa shifted, and her tongue was in my ear. 'Not yet.' Her hand slowed its pounding, and withdrew from its slippery nest. 'I want to feel you come. And I want my face in your fanny when it happens.'

I gasped. She began kissing her way down my body, pausing every few seconds to resume her description of all that she wanted to do, the depths to which her tongue yearned to probe, the swirling and sucking that my own body now ached to experience. With the exception of the occasional finger and, once, the very tip of a dick, I had never … My heart was pounding as I helpfully rolled over, my ass in the air.

She stopped her kissing, her voice a morass of confusion and hurt. 'What? Don't you want me to?'

I froze. 'More than anything.'

80

'So why …' And then we broke down laughing as we each explained what we thought the other one meant, as we discovered that what we Americans call the fanny, the Brits think of as the ass (sorry: arse), and what they call the fanny … I rolled onto my back and spread my legs, as her fingers pulled apart my lips, and her hot tongue scalded the innermost flesh, sought out my clit, winkling it free of its tight little hood and sucking hard on the surrounding flesh.

I cried out. Every nerve in my body seemed to flock for the same tiny spot; each one jostled for the exquisite pressure that left me on the edge of paralysis, but only the edge. My hips bucked, my hands gripped her head, and I came with such force that I had to twist my face into the pillow, simply to stifle the scream.

But Melissa wasn't finished yet. Rather, she flipped me over and, as though there'd been no misunderstanding whatsoever, she parted my butt cheeks and her tongue began sweeping from the base of my spine, all the way down, pausing while two fingers spread my anus wide, and then I could feel her tongue enter me, push its way in, wriggling as it edged deeper, forcing the muscles to relax around it. It was like nothing I'd ever felt. In a way, it wasn't even a sexual sensation; though my pussy still throbbed from the force of my orgasm, this was so different, so gentle, so exquisitely beautiful, as though she'd discovered a whole new way of making love, and all I had to do was lie there and enjoy every moment of it.

Then her fingers were on my clit again, teasing, tweezing, convulsing me with shivers that bordered so close to pain that I finally had to place my hand on her wrist, to slow her movements and redirect her attentions elsewhere, deep inside my vagina. And, when I came again, it was in a screaming, squirting torrent that left Melissa squealing with delight, and reduced me to an exhausted puddle of jelly, flat on my back while my cunt convulsed its final, face-soaking spray, utterly unable to move a muscle.

Melissa lay with me while I recovered. We kissed and cuddled and whispered new secrets, but our night together was already drawing to a close. We both had an early start in the morning, the trade fair was starting at ten, and the flight and the excitement of the day were finally catching up with me. She left around three, and we both apologised in advance for the fact that we might not be able to get so close again all week.

But we both knew that we'd find a way.

No Strings Attached
Elizabeth Coldwell

Amelia decided to mark the last night of the tour by taking to the stage without her underwear. I'd expected her to pull some kind of stunt to grab my attention, but not necessarily this. Oh, it was a clever move. She knew that when she spread her legs, wrapping them possessively around her cello, there was every possibility she'd be giving some lucky members of the audience a teasing glimpse of her bare pussy; just enough to make them wonder whether they'd actually seen what they thought they had.

More importantly, in her usual position on the opposite side of the semi-circle into which our quartet arranged itself every night, she'd be offering the same view to me – and I'd know I wasn't imagining it.

It was the culmination of the flirtatious game she'd been playing since the day we met, showing me what she knew I wanted so badly, and never quite letting me have it.

* * *

Was it really only four months since she'd appeared in my life? I felt as though she'd been haunting me for ever, with her wicked tobacco-roughened laugh and those long legs of hers, tanned the colour of honey. And once the tour was over, she'd disappear as abruptly as she'd arrived, leaving me wondering what might have been if I'd only had the courage to force the issue between us.

Amelia was doing us a favour, and we all knew it. We'd founded the quartet on graduating from the Royal Academy of Music, none of us willing to run the risk of being stuck in the ranks of some second-rate provincial orchestra for the rest of our careers. Heather, the unspoken leader of the group, had come up with our name, Apassionata, and Jill had suggested we dress in something eye-catching and provocative. We'd settled on beaded shift dresses that finished dangerously high on our thighs, given that we performed sitting down. They were in complementary shades of blue. Privately, I worried that we looked like a colour chart for an upmarket range of paints, not entirely convinced of the wisdom of trading on our bodies if we wanted to be taken seriously as musicians. I was wrong, of course; we started getting favourable press attention almost immediately and our concerts were soon selling out as fast as the promoters could put the tickets on sale.

You can't become the hottest girl group on the classical music scene and not enjoy the fringe benefits. Just like rock stars, we attracted our share of groupies, and we didn't always turn their advances down. Liz, who'd always been by far the wildest of us at college, indulged in any number of adventures when we were on tour. On more than one occasion, we spotted her bringing a couple of men back to her room after a concert, and the night we celebrated picking up two awards at a ceremony hosted by the country's leading classical music magazine she celebrated our success by having sex on the balcony of her room, in full view of anyone who might be putting in a late shift in the office block opposite, still clutching a glass of champagne in her hand.

I might have been more discreet, but that didn't mean I didn't enjoy my own share of the fun. Though I didn't broadcast the fact that I was into other girls, enough of them sought me out to make it clear they knew the truth. But though I spent many nights with my face buried in some sexy stranger's pussy, licking till she cried out and clutched tight at my head with her thighs, caught up in the throes of orgasm, or lay back to receive some of the same skilful attention myself, none of these women ever left a lasting impression. I'm ashamed to say I've already forgotten most of their names, let alone which date on the tour they came to. And certainly no one ever got under my skin the way Amelia did.

I'd never have known of her existence if it hadn't been for Heather's accident. Leaving the rehearsal hall where we'd been working on new pieces for what was scheduled to be our most extensive tour yet, Heather slipped on a stretch of icy pavement and broke a bone in her forearm. The doctor who fixed her cast in place assured her the injury wouldn't cause any lasting damage to her playing career, but it did mean we had to find a stand-in cello player or postpone the concerts, something our record company was very much against, given they had scheduled the release of our new album to tie in with the tour. Indeed, it was someone in Harlequin Records' A&R department who recommended Amelia to us. She'd once sent a tape to him, hoping to land a solo deal, and though she hadn't been successful at the time, he still remembered her. 'Talented and gorgeous,' he told us. 'She'd fit in perfectly with the rest of you.'

We weren't so sure, until Amelia walked into the rehearsal room two days later. When she pulled off the oversized woollen hat she'd been wearing, shaking out her long, caramel-streaked curls, I felt a rush of desire, hot and primal, surging down to my crotch. I don't usually fall for someone before they've even opened their mouth, but Amelia was a glorious exception. And when she sat and ran her cello bow across the thick, rosined strings, fingers flying up and down the instrument's neck in a rapid arpeggio, I knew she had the playing ability to back up her outrageous beauty. If she'd been a violinist, and therefore more marketable as a solo artist in the record company's eyes, she'd be a star by now, I was sure of it. As it was, she was a more than adequate replacement for Heather, particularly in my lust-struck eyes.

I did my best to hide the way I felt about her, not wanting to do anything that might upset the well-established equilibrium of our quartet. But I must have been more transparent than I thought, because it didn't take Amelia long to come on to me.

The first time it happened was a couple of nights into the tour, in Southampton. The theatre where we were performing was old, the backstage area small and cramped, with barely enough space for two people to pass each other in the corridor. It gave Amelia the perfect excuse to press up against me, almost as if by accident, as we manoeuvred our instrument cases into the dressing room. I was all too aware of the flirty gleam in her eyes, the feel of her breasts pushing at my own chest. She always went braless under her spaghetti-strapped dress, and her nipples were twin chips of flint, prominent and excited. My response was to murmur some apology for getting in her way, before hurrying into the dressing room, my face flushed and an insistent heat rising in my belly.

She did exactly the same thing on a couple of further occasions, leaving me to stew in an agony of desire and confusion. Each time she went a little further, grinding herself against me in a way that suggested she knew exactly what she was doing, even as she pretended our coming together was simply caused by some quirk of the theatre's design. I'd have thought she was simply toying with me, taking advantage of my unspoken lust for her to have some cruel fun at my expense, if it hadn't been for the fact she seemed just as turned on as I was. Even if she could have achieved the hardness of her nipples by giving them a discreet tweak before ambushing me, the musky scent I always detected in these situations was pure horny woman, impossible to fake – and just as hard to ignore. But she never gave the slightest sign of being outwardly interested in me, or any other woman, and even if she had, I knew the risks I'd be taking by getting so intimately involved with another member of Apassionata, even a temporary one. No wonder my emotions were in turmoil.

As the tour went on, I began to lose interest in the star-struck girls who waited for me after the show, hoping to spend the night in my bed. Sweet and pretty as they were, I didn't want any of them. All I wanted was that bewitching little minx Amelia, and she was strictly off-limits. So each night I retired to my hotel room and dug out my vibrator, letting its thick, rotating shaft and cunning clitoral stimulator bring me to orgasm after orgasm. Face buried in the pillow to muffle the sound of my tormented moans, I would picture Amelia wearing nothing but shiny black thigh-high boots with a thick fake cock jutting from a harness fastened around her waist. In my mind, she used the strap-on to bring me to climax, thrusting hard into my pussy – or, in my kinkiest imaginings, my arsehole – as she ordered me to frig my own clit, only letting me come on her command. The orgasms I had with the aid of that deliciously filthy fantasy were so strong they left me shaking, almost unable to remember where I was for a moment – though that could just have been a natural response to spending every night in some anonymous hotel or other, where the décor and menus were interchangeable and the service always politely detached.

If I'd been in a rock band, I could at the very least have relieved some of my frustration by heaving the television set out of the window, but nice girls in string quartets – even ones who wear teeny-tiny skirts on stage and manage to work instrumental versions of songs by Coldplay and Muse into their concert programmes – aren't supposed to display that kind of uncouth behaviour. So, instead, I continued to put my battery-powered lover through its paces and wished things could be different.

Amelia raised the stakes a little higher the night we played Edinburgh. The mood was particularly poignant, given that we were in Heather's home city; we couldn't help but think of her at home in her flat in North London, still recuperating from her fall, rather than taking the stage in front of an audience including her family and friends, as she'd so been looking forward to doing. Even so, the four of us gave one of the best performances of the tour, as though we didn't want to let Heather down.

Afterwards, with the audience's applause still ringing in our ears, we headed for the dressing room.

'I don't know about you lot,' Jill said, stowing her viola safely in its case, 'but when I get back to the hotel, I'm going to check out the spa, have a soak in the hot tub.'

'Will it still be open at this time of night?' I asked doubtfully. The thought of immersing myself in hot, bubbling water, soothing the tension that made my body feel as taut as the strings on my violin, was an appealing one, but I couldn't see the hotel employing someone to keep the spa open beyond midnight.

'I'm sure they'll keep it open if we ask nicely.' Jill winked. 'Come on, Alex, it's not like we abuse the perks of fame very often.'

She was right; despite my misgivings, the hotel staff couldn't do enough to accommodate us. And when Amelia shrugged off the towelling robe she'd been wearing to reveal the skimpy black bikini she wore beneath it, I forgot about everything but that glorious sight. The tiny triangles of fabric emphasised the gentle curves of her small, high breasts and slender hips, and I hoped Jill and Liz wouldn't notice me staring as Amelia lowered herself in beside me.

The tub was more than big enough to hold all four of us in comfort, but somehow I still found Amelia's body right up against the side of my own, her thigh resting lightly next to mine. Liz had broken the rules by smuggling a bottle of champagne into the spa, and she poured us all a glass before joining us in the water.

She raised her own flute in a toast. 'To us. May the rest of the tour go as well as tonight.'

'They loved us, didn't they?' Jill said, a dreamy expression on her face as she recalled the audience rising in a standing ovation at the end of the concert.

'It's just a shame Heather couldn't have been here,' I pointed out.

'Well, we're lucky Amelia's proved to be such an excellent stand-in.' Jill held her glass aloft again, announcing in mock-solemn tones: 'To Amelia, who really got us out of a hole.'

As I took a sip of my champagne, Amelia murmured in my ear, 'And whose hole you'd really like to get in.'

'I'm sorry?' I said, not sure I'd heard her right.

'Don't act so naïve,' she replied. 'I know how much you want me. But that's OK, because maybe I want you, too.' Again she teased me, not laying her feelings out clearly. She must know she was driving me wild, more so when she slipped a hand beneath the water, letting it settle between my legs.

91

'Amelia, what are you doing?' I kept my voice low, not wanting Jill or Liz to become aware of what was going on, though Liz seemed more concerned with refilling her own glass, and Jill appeared to be lost in her own thoughts, as always.

'Just letting you know how things could be between us ...' As she spoke, she ran her finger lightly over my sex lips, tracing their contours through the material of my scarlet one-piece swimming costume. Even that minimal pressure was enough to have me biting my lip, fighting to prevent a squeak of pleasure from escaping.

'You like that, don't you?' Amelia said. The question was redundant. She couldn't fail to know that even the merest caress had me squirming against the plastic bench seat beneath me, craving more.

I nodded, not trusting myself to speak, my thighs lolling apart as though of their own volition, giving her easier access to what lay between them.

'Just think what we could do if we were alone together,' she continued, her finger finding the little bump of my clit through the stretchy material and stroking it insistently. Her nipples were two hard, visible points beneath her bikini top, and if it hadn't been for the chemical scent of the foaming water, I'd have been able to smell her arousal – and my own. 'My fingers in your pussy, your lips on my clit ...'

Just when I thought she was going to take me all the

way, making me come as the bubbles of the hot tub popped and fizzed around us, she withdrew her hand. Liz was reaching over to offer the two of us more champagne. I was sure, as I held out my own glass, suddenly in desperate need of a drink, that Amelia hadn't stopped touching me because she was afraid of being caught. It was all part of the teasing little game she was playing; a game whose rules I couldn't begin to grasp. In less than a week, the tour would be over, and if I couldn't work out what I had to do to make Amelia mine by then, she'd be gone and I'd have blown the chance for good.

* * *

And now Amelia sat six feet away from me, seemingly oblivious to my presence as she played the 'Sarabande' from Bach's Cello Suite No. 5, her solo spot on our programme. The concert hall was in hushed silence, the audience lost in her passionate performance of this intimate piece. Beautiful as the music was, I didn't hear a note. I couldn't stop thinking of her pussy, bare beneath her short teal dress, and how much I longed to get on my knees and lick the wet, glistening flesh till she convulsed in orgasm.

When she rose to take her bow at the end of the piece, I tried my hardest to look anywhere but directly at her, afraid I'd catch another glimpse of her cunt. Our next piece, a moody Baroque arrangement of George Gershwin's 'Someone To Watch Over Me', was the final number in the first half of the show. I knew that at the interval I'd have to dash to the backstage toilets and make myself come, otherwise I'd be a wreck for the rest of the concert.

Amelia, however, had other ideas. I wasn't aware she'd followed me till I felt her grab my shoulder as I made to enter the toilet cubicle, spinning me round and pinning me to the wall. The functional white tiles were cold against my back, but the rest of my body was overheating as she put her lips close to my ear.

'Did you like my little show?' she asked. She didn't need to elaborate on what she meant. 'I did it for you, Alex, but I'd be lying if I said I wasn't enjoying the feeling. You should try it, being bare for the rest of the concert ...'

Her hand reached up under my skirt. Hypnotised by her soft words and my overwhelming need for her, I made no move to resist. She caught hold of my panties, tugging them right off before dropping them in the waste bin. They were so wet I felt my cheeks flame, ashamed to let Amelia see the effect she had on me.

I expected her to react with a volley of mocking words, amused by my blatant need. Instead, when I raised my eyes, she was looking at me with an expression I couldn't fathom. Then she brought her mouth down on mine in a soft but demanding kiss. For a moment, I almost pushed her away, still believing she was playing some wicked, teasing mind game that would end with me alone and frustrated once more. But Amelia's tongue probed deeper, her fingers meshed in my hair and her belly pressed hard against mine – body language so at odds with my gloomy prediction that I simply stopped worrying about being left high and dry, and responded with a ferocity that surprised me.

I eased one of the thin straps down off Amelia's shoulder, bared her breast and cupped it in my palm. The nipple, already tight, stiffened further under my touch and she moaned into my mouth. Loosing her grip on my hair, she pushed my skirt up around my waist, exposing my naked pussy. She trailed a finger through the little fluff of hair that crowned my mound, then moved lower, into the wet recesses of my cunt, stimulating me just as she'd done in the hot tub. Only now there was no material separating my so-sensitive clit from her gently stroking fingertip.

'You don't know how long I've wanted this,' I murmured.

'Yes, I do,' she whispered back.

'God, you're such a tease ... But I wasn't going to let her tease me any longer. I was going to make sure she gave me what I needed, and provide her with the same pleasure in return. Reaching under her skirt, I slipped a finger into her juicy hole, applied the pad of my thumb to her hooded clit.

If anyone had walked into the ladies' at that moment, they'd have found themselves confronted by two half-naked women, all inhibitions long gone, totally absorbed in the task of touching each other. And if they'd voiced any kind of reaction to the sight, I doubt it would have made us stop what we were doing.

But touching wasn't enough. I needed to taste Amelia, too. I turned her so that now she was leaning against the wall, and dropped to the floor at her feet. Rucking up her skirt, I took my first proper look at what I'd only had the merest flash of before: that sweet, pink pussy, cleanly shaved and slick with her juices.

The tip of my tongue darted out to lick up the pearly nectar, savouring the mixture of salt and sweet that was uniquely hers. One taste wasn't enough, and I lapped more eagerly, exploring the whole length of her slit and even skimming over her anal pucker. That made her shiver, so I lingered there till her legs almost buckled and she begged me not to toy with her any more, but to make her come.

I thought of all my fantasies where the roles were reversed, where I'd been the one at her mercy, and decided I liked this power dynamic just as much. Maybe I'd let Amelia take charge next time – if there was a next time. Pushing that thought way down where it couldn't nag at me, I moved back up in the direction of her clit with a broad sweep of my tongue, feeling more of her juice flood out into my mouth.

'Oh, yes, just there. That's it.' Amelia sighed. 'Don't stop, Alex, whatever you do ...'

Her words tailed off into incoherence, as I set about taking her to the point of no return. I hadn't forgotten about my own need for satisfaction and, as I continued to lick her, my fingers danced over my clit with the delicacy I normally reserved for picking out the notes of a Vivaldi sonata. Moving to a tune I could only hear in my head, an ode to the power of lust and love, I brought first Amelia, then myself to orgasm. Slipping a finger into her cunt in the moment before she came, I felt her walls tighten around it, as though seeking to keep me inside her for ever. Then I reached my own peak, and the world seemed to dissolve for a moment.

When I finally regained full control of my senses, Amelia was staring down at me with a huge smile on her face. She ran a hand through her messy curls.

'Wow!' she sighed, her expression blissful. 'That wasn't part of the plan when I came in here.'

'Oh, and what was the plan, exactly?'

For once, she looked a little sheepish. 'Well, I was intending to get you all hot and bothered ... then, when the concert was over, take you back to my hotel room and fuck your brains out.'

'There's still time for that, surely?'

She nodded, helping me up to my feet. We embraced, enjoying the last, lingering remnants of our shared orgasm, and she dropped a soft, satisfied kiss on the top of my head. Somewhere in the back of my mind, a little voice reminded me that the interval would be coming to an end, if it hadn't already, and that people might be wondering where we'd disappeared to.

'We'd better get back,' I said. 'They'll be needing us for the second half of the concert.'

With some reluctance, we disentangled ourselves before making our way out of the ladies', hand in hand. I was sure that what Amelia and I had started in these less than salubrious surroundings would continue not just tonight but well beyond the end of the tour, and it didn't really matter which one of us was pulling the strings.

Whore-Maker
Scarlett Rush

What if you were a married woman but you wanted to have a quick, dirty and illicit fuck with another girl? I'm not talking about one you had to sneak to a gay club to find. I'm talking about any random, almost certainly heterosexual girl that you just happened upon in the street. Do you have a killer line that you could use to ensnare her in an instant? Something like:

'I don't usually stare at girls but you simply have the most gorgeous eyes I have ever seen and I just can't help myself.'

No, that's all a bit fluffy and toothless isn't it? It's hardly likely to get your target gasping and ripping off her g-string and asking you to shove it in her mouth while you fill her from the rear with anything that comes to hand. What about something more upbeat and direct, like:

'If you're a dyke then I definitely want to plug your hole with my finger – and I'm not even Dutch!'

I'm joking, of course. You might think such a killer line doesn't exist, but you will be pleased to know that I have just the very one up my sleeve and it hasn't failed me yet. It certainly helps if you are as gutsy as me and have the same constantly overwhelming, brain-scrambling, pussy-melting urgency to eat out some sexy bitch until lockjaw sets in. Therefore, if you can summon just a little boldness you will find that the power is all in the words. As long as you pick your target wisely there is no reason why it shouldn't get you what you want every time. My killer line is in fact quite breathtaking in its simplicity and you will wonder why you have never used it before. So, without further ado, here it is (drum roll):

'I will give you two hundred pounds if you let me fuck you.'

Ta-da! Brilliant, isn't it?

But do I sense you are now thinking a much darker edge has tinged what you first took to be a light-hearted subject? Perhaps phrases like 'morally repugnant' are now swirling around your head. Well, before you start to consider the social issues and get all high horse-ish, let me just acquaint you with this single plain fact: two minutes after using my line I get to have a creamy, soft young bottom bent over in front of my face, just like that. The reward for casting principles aside outweighs all. I get to slide my tongue deep into a hot puss and suck out its velvet juices. I get to push my nose hard against a tight, tiny bum-hole and breathe its sweet bum scent. I also get to hear my conquest squeal with the delight of it all, despite herself. Sometimes they even frig themselves off and come, shuddering and squashing against me.

I get to use their body as I see fit. I can rub my saturated quim all over their pale flesh, or force them to slurp me down. I can fill them or have them fill me and no one else will ever know. It will always be hot and urgent, edgy and nasty, and above all it will be addictive in its exhilaration. The monetary figure stated might go up or down depending on the target but the result will always be favourable to both parties, allowing me to put aside the moral issues involved. And when the reality of it all starts to creep up on me I salve my conscience by remembering that it wasn't me that thought the whole thing up in the first place. It was my bastard husband.

* * *

I remember very well the first time I did it. It was a couple of years ago, on my thirtieth birthday. I was in the park feeling lost. I was staring at the no doubt ridiculously expensive bracelet I had been given that day, and thinking of the sham that was my marriage and thus my life. She was sat on the wrought-iron bench opposite. I knew she was a student from the start. I live in a very smart university town, and you learn to spot them a mile off. It was a sunny late spring day and she was in denim shorts, possibly for the first time that year, since her ever so slightly thick legs were alabaster pale and tan-free. She was absent-mindedly chewing on strands of her dark hair and she was lovely enough to make my stomach suddenly flip.

I remembered all the pretty young things that had shared my college days, and all the yearnings to jump upon them that I had so studiously suppressed. I remembered the many naked, fevered, legs-wide-open wanks I had in the secrecy of the dorm, my fingers slapping against my sopping, lust-swollen puss as I imagined stripping one of those girls and fucking her with gay abandon. Back then I thought I had the strength of mind and character to make it happen, but always at the crucial point I faltered, perhaps worried about the scandal if my secret was ever leaked, and the disastrously negative effect that would have on my monthly allowance. So I played the straight woman and never once got to have someone as delicious as her.

Her legs looked so smooth and inviting. I wanted to lick every inch of them, all the way up and up until I was between her thighs and the heat of her was at my open mouth. I could almost taste her. I could picture the incomparable softness of her thighs under my touch. Then suddenly picturing wasn't enough. I remember thinking:

For once, why can't I just have her?

My pussy thought it an entirely reasonable suggestion but my brain knew the realities. Most people don't respond well to being propositioned out of the blue by a stranger. Girls don't suddenly go all lesbian on you just because you flash them a needy smile. If I was a handsome cheeky chappie I might bowl over with some amiable chat and see if I could elicit first a smile and then a phone number. But this wasn't about dating. It was about right-now, no-nonsense, no-questions-asked fucking. No one in this world wilfully surrenders their body like that on a whim. And then I remembered: I did. I surrendered my own body all the time because it suited my cause to do so.

A while back I decided that I no longer wanted my husband's rough, careless hands grasping at my bare flesh. I didn't want his heavy, hairy frame sweating all over me and I didn't want his dirty prick driving artlessly in and out of my body. I basically went on a sex strike. He then decided that if I wasn't going to allow him his conjugal rights then he wasn't going to shore up my ailing business or give me any more access to the substantial funds I was used to receiving from his account. I did a quick rethink and decided that life with him was pretty rough but life with him and penniless was a much graver prospect. So I caved in and gave him what he wanted, all for money. Yes, I really am that shallow!

I now have as much money as I need, providing I lie still for long enough for him to fuck me whenever he wants. I have become his whore, quite literally. And because of my new status he has taken to wordlessly doing things he would never have previously dared to ask of me: spunking hard in my face for instance, or making me stick my finger up his horrid arse. He knows I cannot say no because I am a slave to money and the lifestyle it gives me. I have no power without it, no meaning. He jokes and calls me 'Little Miss Prozzer' in private. He shows me the wad of cash before making me strip. He sometimes scatters my reward over my semen-splurged bottom before giving me a sly smack and a thank-you kiss. He can barely control himself when he gets me acting as his paid hussy and it's entirely possible that he now needs to go through this charade each time in order to get excited enough to perform. He thinks it's all just our little game and perhaps he still has no inkling how much I cannot like him or any of his kind.

To ensure I keep my part he always pays me in cash once I have done him favours. I no longer get any kind of pin money or allowance paid by him directly into my bank. If I want it I have to earn it, and he is blindly under the misconception that I love this arrangement as much as he – such is my willingness to win my reward. I had a couple of thousand pounds of it stuffed into my handbag that day, tossed at me the very morning of my birthday with a smile and a suggestion to buy myself a nice dress to wear to the restaurant he was to take me to that evening.

The money popped into my head and I found myself crossing over toward the student girl. My cheeks were flushed red with the heart-pounding possibility of it all. I felt recklessly potent. I am good-looking for sure, beautiful even, despite my rather stern features. I am pleasing enough to the eye to keep my vain husband thinking he has an enviable trophy to parade, as well as somewhere scrumptious to squirt his ball juice. If I wasn't so damned gorgeous I would never have acquired the nerve to do what I was about to do, but I am. Money adds to what nature provided, so I always look pristine and good enough to eat.

I'm sure I could seduce most straight men rather simply, but to seduce a female was a totally different matter. I needed that same disarming quality that my husband possessed, that innate disregard that made you believe all others were there to do your bidding and could always be bought. I sat next to her and smiled but my head was still throbbing and jumbled, so my opening gambit was clumsy and confusing – something crass about her looks and how I had to have her. She looked stumped. I had nowhere to go except onward, so I took a deep breath and a leaf out of my husband's book, dispensing with the niceties.

'You are making me wet and I have to have you now,' I said. 'I will give you two hundred pounds if you let me take you into those bushes and suck your pussy until you come.'

Well, she had even less to say after that but she was at least rooted to her seat and unable to answer. I felt the bravado rushing through me. She wasn't strong enough to defeat me physically so I was in no danger there. She was stammering her refusals but I could already see the hesitation in her eyes. I upped the ante. I opened my bag and let her see the crisp notes inside. I took a handful and offered it to her, shoved it into her grasp.

'I will give you five hundred, right now, and all you have to do is let me make you come.'

She blinked silently at me, biting her lip and breathing hard. Then there was that beautiful moment that I see every time I do this, when the eyes betray everything. It is just a flicker but it reveals all. It is that instant when your target is swayed, when the moment seems surreal, when the money becomes too good to refuse, when the bargain is suddenly far too good to turn down. An orgasm for money; licked out and made to come by a sexy woman; fucked beautifully and then given a prize too! She gave me that look, the one that says: I want to say no but I just can't make myself. But I can't say yes either, so if you want me you will have to take me ...

Yes, I know that's a lot for one look to say but while

you are pondering the veracity of my words, I was grasping the initiative. I took her and I led her through the screen of bushes and into the woods behind. I had to pull her through the scrub. There were paths nearby and dog-walkers might have been within earshot, but I was damned if I was going to lose my golden chance. I pushed her back against a tree and the breath came from her in a rush. I had to hold her by the wrists since she still had the money clutched in her hand. I leant into her, pulling my short skirt up so that I could plant one bare thigh between her legs to keep them open. Even through her denim I could feel the warmth of her crotch on my skin. Then I kissed her with passion. She was soft and open, warm and wet. She was every bit as luscious as all the girls of my infinite dreams. I pressed into her and her tongue swirled with mine – hesitant at first, but with new urgency as I reached up and pinched her young nipples through her soft cotton vest top.

She put her arms around my waist to hold me but I broke her embrace and dropped to my knees, pulling at her shorts to release their fastening. She was wearing thin peach-coloured knickers, so tight they defined her split beneath. I pulled the material aside and her squashed lips swelled and coloured as they were set free. I remember the exquisite thrill of smelling her excited quim just as I closed my mouth around the plump hood that hid the little pink clit. She let out a gasp and I sucked her. There was no delicacy, only the built-up yearning of way too many years. I sucked just as I would want any girl to suck me: strongly, wetly, mercilessly.

She opened her legs wider and crouched slightly to make sure she was pressed right into me. I slid two fingers up inside her and curled them away from me, pushing against her delicate walls to induce her to squeeze against me. She was trying to suppress her squeals but her excitement was not to be denied and her juices flowed, escaping down my hand and trickling down my wrist, front and back. The feel of warm silky girl-come oozing down my arm remains one of my greatest turn-ons. I waggled my fingers inside her and then turned them around, curling them back towards me in search of her sweet spot. My hunger for her clit grew ever stronger as her lips swelled and softened in my hot mouth. I was remorseless.

I don't know how long I was down on my knees but probably no more than an intense but glorious five minutes. Then she was gripping my hair with her one free hand and grinding into me, whining as she tried to prevent herself from screaming. I was glad she lost herself in those final few moments and showed what a wanton bitch she really was. It made it so much easier for me to leave her there, spent and breathless, with her throbbing clit still dribbling my saliva and the juice shining on her inner thighs. I kissed her again but broke off before she had a chance to cling to me. Then I walked away and left her. My quim was in dire need of attention but there was way too much risk of staying longer in those woods. Plus I wanted to bask in the joy of her puss while I could still taste and even feel its swell in my mouth.

I went home and masturbated until my poor cunny was tired and throbbing, and then I masturbated some more. It wasn't just the joy of eating my first girl. It was also the excitement of knowing that I could have made her do anything, for the right price. That evening I was in no mood for my husband's dirty games but he wanted them regardless. He gave my aching puss a hard birthday fuck. He cried out for joy as he spattered me and then smiled with glee as he threw wads of cash at me and called me his lovely wife-whore. I smiled warmly back at him as I gathered up my hard-earned loot, and thought:

Why, thank you, my darling husband. I'm going to use this money to betray you, you selfish, self-obsessed cunt of a man!

* * *

I never had any choice about who I would end up betrothed to. It was going to be Joshua pretty much from day one. You can call it an arranged marriage if you like, although looking back even I can't remember anyone actually forcing me to wear his ring. It was all done by suggestion and enticement. It was what everyone wanted

109

and everyone knew it would happen, so it just did. Don't think I need any sympathy. I was one of those rich, spoilt daddy's girls who look down on anyone less fortunate. I believed that privilege was my right. My father made sure I had everything I wanted in life, including a fine education. He asked only one thing of me, that I got out of his hair as soon as possible and ensured an even richer man took on the burden of paying for me.

I was always very self-assured and capable of fighting my own corner. After getting my degree the kudos of being a successful businesswoman appealed, but never more than the thought of being a kept woman, with time and limitless resources to do as I pleased. Being paired with Joshua promised a lifetime of just that. I always admired his philosophy of riding roughshod over anyone he chose. It reminded me so much of me. Add to that a veritable Fort Knox-worth of financial resources and he became blindingly attractive to an eligible bachelorette such as my good self. He was like a prince to me then. It's too bad that the thrill of wealth made me forget that what I really needed in life was a princess.

* * *

Having broken my fuck duck with the girlies I reasoned there should be no stopping me. A week or so after my first adventure I returned to the same spot. My ego was a little bruised to not come across my love-struck first conquest searching for me there. Still, I didn't want her cramping my style if I spotted other potential targets. I was armed with cash and a heart full of bravado. A full hour passed without an opportunity arising and I was on the verge of giving up when a plumpish blonde was spotted obliviously texting away in front of a very handy tree-line. She was just about on the pretty side of plain and looked all sweet and studenty in her steel-rimmed glasses. I guessed she would be soft and succulent and too much of a wallflower to protest too much.

'I love sexy young blonde bitches like you,' I told her, without any other introduction. 'I will give you two hundred pounds if you let me suck your pussy dry.'

She was speechless so I filled the silence, telling her precisely what I wanted to do and where I was going to take her to do it. I told her that pale, tight pussies drove me to distraction and I would happily pay her one hundred pounds just to let me see hers. I told her I was more than willing to show her mine in return. I told her that I was even more than willing to double her money if she would just let me make her come. Then I showed her the money and she showed me that look.

She was teetering so I took hold of her and pulled against her minimal resistance until we were blanketed by the trees. I pushed her back against a fat trunk and kissed her to seal the deal and quieten any reluctance.

I pulled up her top and sucked and nipped at her tits through the fabric of her bra. I undid her clasp and released the small handfuls, gorging on them hungrily. I was already dragging at her jeans to try and get them down past her chubby thighs. The fabric clung to her skin and I dropped to my knees impatiently. The waistband had folded over and loose change was dripping from her pockets. The jeans were mid-way down her thighs and my attempts to rid her of them were too clumsy to persist with, so I turned my attention to her tight white knickers and yanked them down.

I gasped as I saw her lovely quim. I thought I had been overstating my love of plump pussies but hers really was a peach – so smooth and utterly delectable. I clamped my lips around the top of her slit and sucked hard enough to make her collapse into me. The press of her softness into my face was divine. I needed to open her up and drink her but her fleshly thighs and unmovable jeans were preventing me. I dabbed and darted at her hole with my tongue but I couldn't find a way in. Even my prodding fingers failed to open her and my amateur efforts were in danger of ruining everything.

Exasperated and red-faced I pulled her down to her knees and quickly kissed her again, then turned her and forced her onto all fours so that her fat cushioned bum was stuck out at me and her pussy was all glistening and needy and right there, bulging between her thighs. I led with my fingers and slipped them into her, smearing her ready juices around her slit and thighs. Then I pressed forward and got my face right in, feeling the give of her bottom against me and the coolness of her cheeks against mine.

I tongued her as deeply as I could as she opened up. I held open the fattened outer lips hiding her little bud and pinched and rolled it between thumb and forefinger, trapping and squeezing her most sensitive spot. She gasped and pushed back against me. I felt the tight knot of her bottom against the tip of my nose and something very dirty in me made me slide my tongue from her depths so I could spit on her delectable arsehole. Then I was burying my face into her again to get her slick wetness all over it. I waggled my head from side to side in my efforts to get ever deeper and she responded by pushing back against me.

I felt her anus against my nose once more but this time my saliva had loosened her. Ever so faintly I could detect her opening up against me. I gripped her thighs hard and pressed on, my tongue aching with its efforts. Christ, yes, it was happening – I could definitely feel it: the slim tip of my ski-jump nose was indeed going into her bottom, fraction by fraction. I don't think I have ever been more excited by anything in my whole life.

I pinched her clit harder and she gave another thrust back, forcing me further into her. Her juice was flowing down my chin but even more blissful was her bum scent now filling my senses. I had breached her arse and got inside. My nose was in her bum-hole and I could actually, beautifully, feel her ring trying to close tight against me, squeezing my nostrils closed. She was squealing and bucking and already way past the point of no return but I gripped her and pinched her and pressed forward, even though my mouth was clamped tight to her puss and I could no longer breathe through my nose. The air was spent in my body and my head was beginning to cloud and throb but I held her and held her as the climax ripped through her luscious flesh and made her shake.

I wanted her to lick me afterwards, but she was too exhausted and dazed. I had her by the hair and was telling her to stuff my pussy full of her fingers but she just stared doe-eyed at me and told me I was beautiful. In the end I couldn't bear it. I was raging with rudeness and needed to spend it. I grabbed more money from my bag and thrust it into her hand. I put my face in hers and told her to suck my nose. I felt the warmth close over me and her tongue lapping my skin. I had my hand down in my knickers and I did myself, frigging wildly as she sucked and licked her own pussy- and bum-taste from my face. I don't know exactly how much she earned from me in those few frantic minutes but it was worth every penny and more of my husband's money. I left her there just as I had left my first conquest. Two steps out of our hiding place and I was already buzzing with the need to find another target and do it all again.

When your husband is such a full-on pompous shitbag it is hard to admit that he's right, but he was. There was something unequivocally exhilarating about buying someone for your own ends. For me the thrill was not just in the sex but in the potential of it. When my nose had slipped up Chubby Blonde's arse I pretty much reached my nirvana. With the delicious rudeness of it there came a rush of thoughts about what else I could do, about how I could stick my thumb up there if I wanted. Or even, dare I say it, my tongue. I had bought the right. There could be no repercussions, no awkwardness afterwards, because it was not love but a simple transaction. I could be as dirty as I dared and then leave the scene scot free to return to my comfortable reality.

As I lay there wanking after that second time a horde of unspeakable images bombarded my mind, some of which I doubt I could ever bring myself to do to another girl. But the point was I could if I wanted. While I fucked my bought bitch I could let imagination take wings. Anything I wanted could be mine. Once they had caved in it was just a matter of how much needed to be paid in exchange for each new depravity. The bottom line was that I was now fully addicted to girls' bums and needed more immediately.

I therefore needed more money. Wasting even a second trying to rekindle the embers of my forgotten business was pointless. It was unthinkable to spend any time whatsoever bullshitting to some stuck-up hag about which ridiculously patterned wallpaper and emu-leather scatter cushions I could supply to transform her tasteless penthouse into a home to die for. Generating wealth myself would be a tiresome, frustrating waste of my precious life. No, I just needed my husband's cock inside me, and to be paid for it.

I actually started playing him at his own game. As my lust for female flesh grew, the need to entice him became ever more important. When the park stopped yielding enough potential targets I trawled the area for better sites. Supermarkets became my prime hunting grounds, particularly the more down-market ones. They were always built out of town, so surrounding wasteland or woodland was easy to find. Failing that, I could use my car and simply drive my girl to a secluded part of the giant car parks. Best of all, there was always a plethora of potential targets, all day long. I would stake out the area then go home fizzing with excitement and squeeze into a corset to bait my tongue-lolling dog-on-heat fool of a husband. I started relatively small. If he didn't fall for my scantily clad seduction technique I would start his fire by saying something along the lines of:

'Give me two hundred and I will suck your cock dry and drink all your come.'

Bizarrely, I rather came to enjoy my efforts. While I was performing for him I would be turned on by what dirty things his money would buy for me. I was even turned on by the thought of what was going on in his head, of all the filthy things he no doubt wished to buy from me. My brain would be thinking: I wonder if he wants to spank me. I wonder how much he would pay for that. The more I thought about which rude things I could charge him for, the dirtier my thoughts became towards the girls I targeted, and thus my need to get more money out of him increased.

Having had one girl's fulsome arse in my face, I sought more. I targeted the girls with fatter rumps – never hard to find these days, thank goodness! I told them plain that I wanted to stick my face in their bent-over behind, and I told them how much I would pay them for it. Generally I wanted to make them come but gradually my own needs began to take precedence and I would always finish each snatched session with my knickers down and either their fingers or my own inside my streaming quim. Once my orgasm was attained, we were done.

I grew to love the council-estate girls with tarty make-up and their gaudy tight clothes hugging their plump arses. Most of all I loved them for their no-nonsense approach to my propositions. At the outset they would nearly always curse at me or threaten me. Then they would very often haggle. Then they would give themselves up. Sometimes

117

they would even offer 'extras' to boost their bounty. One girl even undercut her friend after I brazenly approached both of them. She said she would do it for one-fifty and then bent over a low wall with her leggings and panties down to seal the deal. She nonchalantly smoked as I did her, and told her usurped friend throughout what a filthy lesbo cunt I was. Hers was the first arse I ever licked. She was so dirty and rude I just couldn't help myself, and it earned her an extra fifty. She tasted bitter-sweet and earthy and I just adored the rudeness of it.

Very soon I became addicted to having girls sit on my face and grind their bottoms into me. I already loved the way I could push into them from the rear until all oxygen ran out. Then I took it a step further, wanting to take it to the brink so that I was in danger of suffocation as I licked them. It was a glorious way to build an intense rush within the limited time allowed. I even began taking a smooth dildo out on my whoring missions so they could fuck me furiously as they smothered me, bringing me to a huge climax as I came close to passing out. Since I was upping my demands on my targets I had to increase the rewards, which meant ensuring my pleasantly surprised hubby always had good reason to open his fat wallet. He would thus come home to find me with my legs apart and a dildo already inside my oiled puss, or with a ball gag in place, or wearing a vest top upon which was scrawled in red lipstick a

118

'menu' of the services I was prepared to offer and the price for each.

I began to build a reputation amongst the estate girls I hunted. New girls would hear the rumours and crop up at my usual haunts hoping to attract my business. I could not get enough of them. For a while I achieved a balance in extracting enough from my husband to feed my near mania to seek out girls and pay them for the use of their bottoms. I felt like just another crack whore, or more specifically an arse-crack whore. Fortunately, hubby Josh was uncharacteristically slow to abuse the power he now had over me. By using my imagination I could appease him by chucking new things into the mix. I would masturbate while sucking him, for instance, and then wipe my juice-wet fingers down my face. He would get all bubbly and beside himself and chuck another wad my way. I was just about in control of things.

And then I met Louise.

There is no such thing as love at first sight. It is a nonsense concept spouted only by the shallow. However, with Louise it was well and truly love at first sight. It is pointless trying to describe her prize ass-et and do it justice; suffice to say that it is fat in a glorious way, all sticky-out, satin-smooth and softer than you could dare hope. She flaunted it in her very tight leggings and high-heeled shoes. Worse still she was very pretty. She had me over a barrel in seconds. I loved her jet-black bob and full crimson lips, her thick eye-liner and blusher-cut pale cheeks. She was luscious and she knew it. I think she was almost expecting to be propositioned. Even as I approached she had a faint smile that said:

I know you want me.

I did. More than anything, I really did. She was standing with a trolley full of groceries, smoking and nonchalantly chewing gum as she waited for her overweight, under-dressed chavvy friend to finish some heated, foul-mouthed phone conversation. Louise was tough for sure. Every cell of her was bursting with self-confidence. As I approached she fixed me with her unflappable gaze and I quickly had to remember my mantra: everyone bows to money. I was surely invincible as a whore-maker but still my heart jumped into my mouth.

Despite all my previous successes I heard my faltering voice tell her how wet I was for her, and how I would give her FOUR hundred to let me make her come. Her lack of shock suggested she was well aware of my reputation. If so she should have been flattered that I had doubled my now customary opening bid just for her. However, she just leant back, incredulous, looking me up and down with raised eyebrows. She chewed her gum with open-mouthed rapidity to let me know how undaunted she was by my audacity. I thought briefly that she might spit it out into my face. Just as well she didn't as my legs were too jellified to run and I might have just crumbled into a heap before her. Finally she looked back into my eyes and said, 'You mean five hundred, don't you?'

FIVE hundred? For a trashy, war-paint-drenched, belly-button-pierced, benefit-scrounging young floozy like her?

'Yes,' I said.

She took this renewed offer with a simple shrug. I was told I would have to take her home after. There was a park on the way and we could do the dirty deed there. The friend was left still haranguing her phone caller and I led Louise away as if I were a plain-clothed detective taking her into custody. The friend didn't seem in the least bit perturbed. My blood was rushing so much I could barely see on that short journey. Louise sat in the passenger seat and lit up another cigarette without asking permission, casually eyeing the passing scenery as if she did this kind of thing every day. At one point she opened her legs slightly and gave her tightly-covered pussy a little squeeze and a rub.

I gabbled dirty stuff at her, about how sexy her arse was and how I wanted her to shove my face in it so I could stick my tongue right up it. She just laughed at me and called me a desperate dyke bitch. She showed me where to park and led me up into some trees to the perfect hidden spot. It was obvious she had used this place before. I thought she would just hang back and make me do all the running, but instead she instigated proceedings, teasing me by turning to stick her bottom out, then slowly peeling down her leggings to expose her pink g-string and her delicious creamy soft buttocks. I was told to hand her the money and only then did she get on all fours, bottom fully out and waiting for me.

I was lost in her way before I sank to my knees behind her. I could smell her sweetness as I kissed the flawless expanse of rump. I took down her knickers and she tucked in the small of her back to make her bottom yawn for me. Her little hole was perfection itself. For all her apparent indifference she was river-wet and my fingers slipped into her warm pussy with ease. I waggled them fast inside her, hoping to take her breath away and make her want me. She just counted out her reward. I was slapping my fingers in and out of her squashy puss and she was taunting me with:

'Twenty, forty, sixty ... stick your fingers right up me, you filthy tart ... eighty, one hundred ...'

I buried my face into her, thrusting my tongue deep into her wet slit. She tasted slightly honeyed, slightly metallic. Her pussy lips were so delicate, so slick-smooth, it was almost unbearable. I wanted to eat her cunt, quite literally. Her bum-hole was at my nose and it smelled like chocolate. I exclaimed this – don't ask me why. I came up for air to pay her this silly compliment and all she did was look back over her shoulder at me and sneer, because I was acting like such a lost, desperate idiot. I tried to regain the ascendancy. I pinched at the skin of her pussy around her clit and used other fingers to fuck her, and I ate out her arse with more greed than ever before. She held herself open and pushed out to aid me. God, she tasted beautiful. She felt beautiful. I wanted her to cry out that she loved me but what she actually said was:

'Oh, you fucking dirty whore!'

Her words sucked the last remnants of power from me. I wanted to ravish her but I couldn't bear the thought that she didn't feel something for me in return, that our coupling was cold and emotionless. I needed to regain my strength. I smacked her bouncing bum and then bit and sucked in mouthfuls of the beautiful flesh. Still she cursed me and called me a dirty bitch. I felt the blood bubbling through my body with my shame and frustration that I was doing this to her, not for her, and that I couldn't make her want me as much as I now seriously wanted her.

She was starting to give out a low moan as my fingers danced inside her. The juice was pouring from her puss, bathing my palm and wrist. Her bottom was quaking, tiny little mesmerising shudders that made me want to gorge on her flesh once more. I found myself checking the urge, afraid that she might mistake my specific desire for her for mere general wantonness. Instead I plunged my face back in and forced my tongue-tip back into her slippery bottom. Through her gasps she managed to hiss:

'Make me come, you dirty arse-licking whore!'

Her suppressed squeals were the most exhilarating sounds I had ever heard. The squelch of her pussy and the flow of her excitement down my skin made me want to scream for, well, I don't know what for. My head was nearly bursting with the throb. There was lust mixed with pride at bringing this luscious girl to climax, plus a wrenching sense of detachment. I was making her come, but I was nothing to her. I felt almost violated by her indifference.

The need for some kind of greater connection proved too strong. While she was still coming I took my cum-slippery fingers from her pussy and pushed them into her arse. Don't ask me why I did it. Maybe it was through some hopeless need to own her bum. She screeched and her head snapped back. I had used three fingers, not just the two that were in her puss. I had scrunched them together to make a point of sorts, and they had only gone up her defenceless bottom to the middle knuckle, but my face was burning with the shame of my action and the blood was bubbling through me once more. It had magnified her climax two- or three-fold but she glared back over her shoulder at me with contempt for having the boldness to use her in such a dirty way.

Her disdain ripped at me. I wanted to either make it right or enforce my supremacy. Without thinking I fished for my bag, found a few more banknotes and unceremoniously pushed them up her pussy. I had a stupid sneer on my face to show it was just a joke. I wanted her to smile and cuddle me and say that the money was just a kinky game we played between us to make us hot. I wanted her to understand that in paying her I was just providing her with a legitimate excuse to do all the dirty things I asked of her. Instead the money was being extracted and put with the rest and her clothes were being yanked back up. I stayed on my knees, my chest heaving. I needed to hold her, to gather her in and claim her. I needed to kiss her, but as I got up to embrace her she was already lighting another cigarette and blowing smoke into my face with a taunting laugh.

She barely spoke to me as I concluded our bargain by driving her home. She spoke instead into her phone, arranging a night out to get drunk, eyeing the money in her bag that would enable her to have a ball. As she was leaving I had to blurt out over her on-going conversation that I wanted, I needed, to see her again. She chewed her gum and looked me up and down once more. In the end she assented and I was told to go to the same parking area at the same time the next week.

'Make sure you bring enough money,' she said. 'I'm going to cost you everything you have.'

I won't bore you with the whole week-long wanky maelstrom I went through before our next meeting. In short, I couldn't wait. I spent hours just lying there dreaming of kissing her incomparably soft lips. The smell of her was in everything, the taste of her always sadly elusive. My husband didn't know what hit him that week. I screwed every last penny out of him, hoping it would be enough to earn Louise. I gave up everything to him for money, including my own precious bottom which I had steadfastly always refused him, given up for a measly thousand. I reasoned it would be worth it.

I parked up and saw her standing away by the trees. My bag was full of cash. I was willing to give her the thousand my bum had yielded just to have hers in my face. I also had another thousand in reserve, not to give but to flash around to entice her to keep up our meetings indefinitely.

As soon as I followed her into the trees I knew something was wrong. I was facing her in the little clearing we had previously used. She was smiling at me. Beside her, also with a smug grin, was her chubby chav friend from the supermarket. Then behind me more estate girls were emerging from their cover to surround me. I recognised many faces, although most of these girls would have been bare-arsed and bent over the last time I saw them. The ring closed in on me and I wasn't going to buy my way out of this one.

Louise ordered me to give her my bag and I mutely did. Then she told me to hand over my jewellery. I started to protest but she just raised her eyebrows and held out her hand. Behind me the girls clamoured closer.

She took everything, my watch, the birthday bracelet, my wedding ring. Then she ordered me to strip. When I was too slow the girls moved in to help me. As each garment was yanked off the girls squabbled to claim it as their own. When I was naked the insults started. Louise just stood there smirking as the rest called me all the dirty names under the sun. I tried to stand tall but my legs were quaking.

I wanted to cry, to tell her to send the rest away so we could sort it out between us, because I wanted her and only her. But she already had my money and all the power I ever held. She told me to get down on the floor and I obeyed. I lay on my back and Louise slowly lowered herself down upon me. I could see the black cotton of her leggings stretching over her bum as it descended towards my face. Despite my predicament I would still rather have been there than anywhere else. The weight came down and smothered me. I could taste her clothes and smell her warmth. I heard her tell the girls to go ahead and teach this dirty whore a lesson.

The contact was hesitant at first – a few light tugs on my nipples, slaps at my outer thighs. But then Louise herself pinched my nipples hard and that signalled the frenzy. I was bitten, pinched and sucked. Slaps came to my breasts and stomach, and then, as my legs were twisted to the side, to my buttocks also. Soon the hard spanks were also being aimed at my pussy.

I had to fight for air beneath Louise and my cries were fruitlessly muffled. Fingers were going inside me, not one at a time, but in their twos and threes. I couldn't stop them, not with my pussy weeping its juices like never before. I could feel the wet impact of the girls' spit and the rivulets of it dribbling down my skin. I could feel hot, stinging slaps at my burning puss each time it was emptied of fingers. I even felt a warmer liquid rush splashing right at my opening, accompanied by cheers and taunts from my ravishers.

Amid the tumult Louise tugged at her leggings and her soft bare flesh was suddenly against me. My mouth and nose were pressed into her delicious crack. She was grinding into me and I could hear her demands to be licked. Despite the abuses aimed particularly at my puss, I still automatically flung my thighs apart and raised my hips off the floor, my stiffened clit seeking attention to match the pleasure of her bottom in my face. I felt her hands behind my knees, helping me stay open. I could smell her sweetness. My tongue slipped from her dripping cunt and sought her little anus. The taste of it was instantly identifiable. It was chocolate. Not the sort-of chocolate of her natural taste, but actual chocolate. She had obviously prepared for this encounter by taking a dollop of melted chocolate and smearing it around her lovely bum-hole, just for me. Just for me!

Despite the slaps and pinches, the bites and the spitting, it was bliss. As I yearned to be filled like the whore I

128

unquestionably was, fingers went to my puss. They were pressed together at the tips, like mine had been when I pushed them into Louise's bottom. They parted my slick lips and eased inside. I began to yell but the soft bottom just came down and smothered my noise. I was stretched open, not just by fingers, but by the thumb also, by the whole hand, remorselessly easing me open until the whole fist was inside me, and I was shaking and coming and close to fainting.

When I finally came to I was alone. It took many more minutes before I could even get to my knees. I was naked and all my clothes and possessions were missing. Only my car keys remained, lying on the stump of a sawn tree trunk. The strange roughness I felt in my pussy proved to be from the single five-pound note that had been shoved inside it. Payment for services rendered, no doubt.

When I had gathered enough strength I had to run nude to my parked car. It had been spray-painted. The phrase 'arse-licking lesbo whore' was scrawled all down one side. I had to drive naked to my house, through the traffic of the town, with my indignity displayed to all. I had to scramble around at the front of my house to find the spare key, whilst a group formed to jeer and abuse me. They had seen the words sprayed upon my car. They were still loudly demanding to know how much I charged when I finally managed to close the door against them and find sanctuary.

I am still sitting here now, naked and shaken to the core, my legs barely able to move. But they have to. Somehow I have to get up and get that car out of the drive and have it cleaned before my husband sees it. How I will do that with no money in the world is anyone's guess, but I must. If I don't I am done for and it all falls down. How can I explain those words? How can I explain the scratches and marks all over my body, and the loss of my jewellery? He won't want me once he realises just how much of a whore I've made of myself. He will throw me out without a penny to my name, and with only one way that I know to earn a crust.

My marriage is a farce but I need to cling to him and his money because I am ruined without its comfort. Worse, I need his wealth to continue to feed my ever spiralling addiction. My drug is the filthiest sex with the most immoral girls. Normal sex won't do it for me any more. I can't have simple kissing and stroking and tenderness. I have to own them. I need to use them in such a depraved manner that the only way they can agree to my demands, no matter how much the thought of it secretly turns them on, is to be paid for it. Offering money is the only way I have to gather the courage to proposition them. How the hell else am I going to get gorgeous, trashy estate girls to squash their luscious chubby arses into my face until I pass out?

I am addicted to Louise and all of her kind. I am trembling just thinking of her name. My fingers are deep inside me just picturing her peachy, perfect rump. My shame is immeasurable. I try to get upstairs to get dressed but I can't even make it past the fruit bowl. I have to feed my frenzy by sitting, legs open, on the floor and pumping a banana in and out of my saturated cunt. I have to sate my craving by pressing my big tits together and furiously lapping and slurping at my cleavage, trying to imagine it is her arse crack I'm licking. That's how lost I am.

I don't care what I have to do to taste her again, or any other bum as beautiful. I will commit any indignity to have those girls gang-fuck me, pinch and spank and fist me, smother me with their dirty arses. I am almost shaking apart with the dread of never being able to afford Louise again, but I have to cling to hope, no matter what it costs me. I will surely explode if I don't get her softness in my face again soon. I will do anything she demands of me. I will pay literally any price at all just to lose myself once more in her delectable chocolate-tasting bum.

I Obey Her
Valerie Grey

As I went up the stairs to the dorm, my stomach clenched. Karin was in the room, waiting for me. The first thing she said: 'Pants down, darling. I want to see what's *mine*.'

'Do I have to?' I asked. I was expecting a different greeting – a kiss, a hug, something tender, not this.

Karin said, 'Only if you still love me, darling.'

I took a deep breath and undid my jeans and pushed them and my panties down, baring myself to her. Then I bent over and grabbed my ankles, knowing what was coming.

'Take them off completely, Sloane, so you can move your feet further apart. It'll give you better balance, darling.'

I obeyed her, knowing as I bent over again that my cheeks spread and Karin was eyeing my pussy and asshole.

'Grip tight, Sloane.'

I did and then I heard that sound that was still familiar to me: the whoosh of the strap just before it impacted my bare ass. I bit my lip to keep from howling. Karin hit me with the strap another five times.

'Your ass sure *jiggles* when I hit it. And it turns such a nice shade of red. I *love* how your ass cheeks clench every time I spank it. But what is the *most* enjoyable thing is how your cunt gets wet. On everyone else, it's a vagina or a pussy, but on you it's a *cunt*, isn't it?'

I couldn't answer.

'*Isn't* it, Sloane?'

I said, 'Yes, it's a cunt, Karin.'

'And *whose* cunt is it?'

'It's your cunt.'

'Do you have a bra on, darling?'

'Yes.'

'It's not appropriate attire when you are with me. Take it off.'

I shivered and removed my top and then my bra, and stood naked except for my shoes. Karin took my bra and bent and picked up my panties and tossed them into the closet.

'Turn around.'

I did so and Karin slapped my ass softly. Then she reached up with both hands and pinched and rolled my nipples until they were hard and sticking out.

'Get dressed, time to eat.'

We left the dorm and went to the Commons for lunch.

* * *

She said, 'Let's go back to the room. I have something in mind for you.'

We walked back to the dorm building, enjoying the warmth and sunshine. We got there shortly and climbed the stairs to our floor. As we reached the landing, Karin stopped me.

'Take off your shoes.'

I was curious, but I did as I was told. Once they were off, Karin moved them away from me. She reached towards me, took hold of my top and pulled it up over my head and off.

'Karin, what are you doing?' I asked.

'I thought about this; I thought about it a lot. I want to *show you off*. I want people to *see* you naked; I *really* do.'

One hand reached for my shorts and unbuttoned them; Karin slid my zipper down. Just that fast my shorts felt very loose on me. She held them up against me. She took her other hand and tilted my head.

She said, 'You *want* to make me happy, don't you, Sloane? You *really* want to make me happy, *don't* you?'

All I could do was nod. I glanced to the stairs and saw that I was in plain sight of anyone who reached the landing below. I looked down the hall towards our room and it seemed like it was miles away. Karin released her grip on my shorts and lightly pushed on them. I felt them slide down my legs and puddle around my ankles – once I stepped out of them I would be totally naked in the dorm, in the hallway.

'Give them to me,' she ordered.

I bent and slipped out of my shorts and hesitantly handed them to her. She picked up my top and shoes.

'Count to fifty, then you can come to the room.'

Karin turned and walked away, leaving me bare-assed in the hall. I was so shocked I didn't even think to start counting. When I finally realised that I needed to count, I started but I was nervously shifting from one foot to the other as I imagined another girl with her parents in tow, turning the corner to the landing below and then seeing a naked girl standing at the top of the stairs. I glanced over my shoulder to look down to the landing and then saw the large window that faced the boys' dorm just across the way. I had only by now reached twenty. I shivered and kept counting. When I finally reached fifty I began to walk down the hall to our room. I could feel my breasts bouncing slightly on my chest and the jiggle of my ass behind me. As I walked I could imagine several boys looking out their room windows and seeing me naked in the window in my dorm. I flushed. I reached our door and knocked softly.

'Karin, may I come in, please?'

The door opened and Karin stood there, looking me up and down. She reached out and tweaked both of my nipples.

I let out a soft cry, a moan.

She stepped back and I scurried into the room.

'How do you feel?' she asked.

'Scared, really warm, tingly all over,' I answered.

'Good. Get on my bed. You know the position, slut.'

I hurried over to obey and got on my hands and knees, waiting for her. I knew what was coming. I heard her rustling in one of her suitcases, then I felt her climb up behind me. I felt her rub a rubber cock over my pussy lips and then the tip was at my hole and she slowly slid it up me. I groaned as she filled me. She slid it into me until the base hit my lips and she held it there.

'Does it feel *good*, slut? Do you crave a cock up your cunt?'

'I want you to fuck me every chance we get, darling,' I replied softly.

She wiggled her hips from side to side and slowly slid back out of me, making me whimper. I felt so empty after being filled so deliciously. Karin drove her cock up me hard and I gave a little gasp and held onto the comforter on her bed as she fucked me. In the midst of the fucking, I felt lube dripped on my asshole and moaned. I knew she was going to fuck my ass too. I was pushed forward as she thrust up me and then moved back as she pulled back. I felt a thumb or finger go up my ass and groaned out loud. As much as I wanted to please Karin, I still didn't really like having my asshole penetrated, but it wasn't as if I had a choice with her. If I struggled, she would just hold me down until she got her cock up my asshole anyway.

She fucked me hard for several minutes and then she pulled out of my cunt. Up until now Karin had been silent. 'Where does my cock go *now*, slut?'

I mumbled, 'Up my asspipe.'

'*Good* girl.'

I felt the tip at my asshole and Karin pushed firmly and steadily until it was lodged inside. With a slow and steady pressure she slid it right up until I felt the base on my butt cheeks.

'Where's my cock *now*, you dirty fucking *whore*?'

'In my asspipe,' I muttered.

'What's it *doing* in your asspipe, cunt?' as she slowly pulled back.

'Fucking my ass, Karin, *fucking my asshole*.'

She grabbed my ass cheeks and slid back up me and then back out and in and back, going faster and faster until the sound of her hips hitting my butt cheeks was like slaps.

'Rub your clit and *come*, you dirty *cunt*.'

I reached back with one hand and started rubbing my pussy and clit frantically and as I did my head and chest slumped down to the comforter, lifting my rear end higher. Karin didn't lose rhythm; she kept fucking like a machine. I was moaning and rubbing harder and harder until I came, ramming my butt hard against her. Karin pumped her cock in and out and clutched my cheeks so hard it hurt and then I felt her jerking against me as she came also. When her spasms ceased she collapsed on top of me and I ended up flat on my belly with her cock still jammed in my asspipe. I could feel her hard nipples against my back; her breath came hot and heavy on my neck. She rolled off me and her cock pulled out of me, leaving my asshole gaping open.

'Kiss me, darling, and then you can take off the dick and wash it. You don't have to suck it clean today.'

I rolled to her and kissed her lips lovingly and then knelt up and removed the strap-on. Karin was just as naked as I was now and she looked so lovely to me I couldn't believe that she was with me. I bent over and kissed each of her nipples and then her slit and got up and went to the bathroom to clean the dildo. Even after being ass-fucked I was so happy it seemed unreal. Everything I wanted I had here, our splendour in the dorm.

I just hoped that she felt the same way.

She said, 'Go take a bath. Then come back here.'

'I don't have towels out yet.'

'I'll find them, just go and wash up like I told you and then come back here.'

I walked into the bathroom, filled the tub and luxuri-
ated in it for a few minutes, and then I washed up quickly
and went back to the bedroom, dripping water. When we
had first moved into this room there were no curtains on
the big window, but once we had started making love,
Karin had bought some. The curtains were closed most
of the time, but now the curtains were pulled back and
I could see the boys' dorm across the courtyard. I moved
to the window to close the curtains.

'No, Sloane. Leave them open.'

I looked at her, shocked by this.

She said, 'Step right in front of the window, darling.
Then you can have a towel.'

I shivered. I stepped over so I was partially in front
of the open window.

'More,' Karin told me.

I hesitantly took another step to my right and now
I was in the centre of the window with the curtains
pulled back. Karin stepped up where I had been, hidden
from any eyes that might be looking at our window. She
handed me a towel.

'Dry yourself off, darling, just as if the window isn't there.'

I held the towel in front of me and briskly dried my
arms.

Karin giggled. 'Turn around to dry your front.'

I did as I was told, but before I turned, I looked
down. The window sill was slightly above my knees so

from there on up I was totally exposed. Shivering again, I turned so my entire bare back and bare ass faced the window. Then something happened that I certainly didn't expect.

'Hello, Jeremy? Are you at your window? You *are*? Good. What can you *see*?'

She was talking on cell her phone to a guy!

'You can see a *bare ass*? Great! Do you *like* it? Is anyone else there with you? Oh, *that's wonderful*! Five of you, eh? Do *they* like what they're seeing too? Great! Oh, just stay there and watch. It'll be a *treat*. Bye.'

I mindlessly rubbed the towel on my flesh ...

I couldn't believe Karin was doing this to me.

'Bend over and get your legs, darling.'

I slowly bent over and dried my legs and feet and my imagination was going wild. I closed my eyes and imagined five guys clustered around a window in the dorm and then my view trailed across the lawn between the two dorms and up to our window. And there I was, exposed from my knees to my head. My bare ass was reddened from the strapping I had received.

'I think your front is done, Sloane. Turn around and do your back now.'

'Karin, *please*, I don't ...'

She glared at me. 'I really don't *care* what you want or *don't* want. What *I* want is for you to turn around and dry your back, *right there, right now*. I don't want

140

to *hear* any backtalk from you. I just want you to do as you are *told*.'

I turned around. I slid the towel over my shoulder and grasped the lower end with my other hand. I began to slide it over my back. My nipples were erect once more and further down was my bush and it was wet, not just from water.

This was turning me on and I didn't want to believe it was turning me on.

Karin spoke into her phone: 'Hi, Jeremy. You *can*? Yes, she does have little tits, but her nipples look right now like they could *cut glass*. Yes, she does have a little too much hair, but that can be taken care of, too. Even so, you *like* what you're seeing, don't you? Great! No, I am *not* going to start a schedule for you and your friends. You are just going to have to look out from time to time. I can promise you that this won't be the last time.'

I was ashamed and aroused at the same time; I hated it and I loved it. I wanted to crawl into a hole and I wanted to pose for them. What *was* this about me?

'Sloane, darling, toss the towel on your bed and do a little turn for me. All the way around, right there.'

I looked at her, at the heat in her eyes as she stared at my naked body, and without really thinking about it at all I tossed the towel onto my bed and slowly turned so my breasts were in profile, then my ass was dead on the window, then my breasts in profile once more and then full-on frontal, right there in front of the window. I was hot and bothered. I was totally aroused. I wanted to touch myself, to masturbate and tweak my nipples. I glanced at Karin and she was slipping her strap-on up to her hips, fastening it in place. She lay back on her bed with her cock sticking straight up and crooked her finger at me. I moved away from the window and to her bed, crawled up, straddled her, grasped her cock, set it at my pussy and slid down it until my ass was on her thighs and her cock was buried inside me as deep as it could get.

'Fuck me, you dirty bitch! Move that slut ass and *fuck me*!'

I closed my eyes and grasped a breast with each hand and without thinking about it at all, my hips started swinging forward and back, fucking her as fast and as hard as I could.

'*Move your hands, slut!*'

I dropped my hands down and Karin grasped my breasts and squeezed them, pinching and rolling my nipples. She lay there as my ass swung forward and back, fucking as hard and as fast as I could. With my pussy full of cock and my clit rubbing on her it wasn't long before I was gasping, so close to coming it almost hurt. Then Karin let go of my breasts and grabbed my hips and began to buck up and down. Now she was fucking me and my vision blurred and I exploded. My head fell back and my body shuddered as my orgasm roared through me. Karin pounded up into me all the way through my spasms and then she climaxed underneath me, her strokes becoming ragged but still forceful. When her orgasm tapered off I slumped forward and she grabbed me and pulled me down on her.

'Was it good for you, darling?' she asked.

'It was wonderful, amazing. One of the best I have ever had,' I whispered.

'So, you don't *like* showing off, huh? I *wonder*.' She giggled and pushed up inside me once more. '*Twice* in two hours, slut. Do you think you can do it again tonight?'

'I think so, Karin. I think so.'

'We'll just have to *see*, then, *won't* we?' She kissed my cheek and held me and we both fell into a doze.

* * *

We got dressed and went to the Commons for dinner. Two girls walked up and I tensed. Ashley and Jenny – they had both seen me naked; one time they had seen Karin fuck me and then she let Jenny fuck me too. Then I ended up fucking Ashley. It was something that made me a little sick to my stomach when I remembered it. It was something that I wished had not happened ... but it did.

Jenny asked, 'What are you two going to do now?'

'Just going back to our room,' Karin said and winked.

'Can we come along?'

'Sure,' Karin said with a devious smile.

I got a nervous feeling in the pit of my stomach but I didn't say anything. We went to our dorm building, which was also Ashley and Jenny's building – they lived on the third floor. We walked up the stairs and once we reached the landing on our floor, Karin turned to me and said, 'What are you supposed to do, darling?'

'Can we not today, Karin?' I asked softly.

'I don't want you to start getting bad habits,' she said seriously.

Both Ashley and Jenny were looking at me, wondering. I took a deep breath. It wasn't as if they would see anything new. I just didn't like it. I toed off my shoes and pulled my top over my head and handed it to Karin. I undid my shorts and slid them down my legs and off. I bent over, picked up my shoes and shorts and handed them to Karin.

'Oh *wow*!'

Two pairs of eyes were focused on me. Actually three pairs of eyes, but one pair I didn't mind. Jenny turned to Ashley.

'I think that this is a *great* idea,' Jenny said. 'Ashley – *strip*!'

Ashley was shocked. 'You *can't* be serious!'

'You bet your sweet ass I am. And I wanna see *that ass* naked like Sloane and everything else, *right now*! If

144

you don't, we'll discuss this when we get back to our room. *Now get your clothes off.*'

Ashley closed her eyes (just like I do) and slipped off her shoes. Kind of funny how the shoes go first almost all the time. Ashley pulled her top over her head and then undid and slipped her shorts off, leaving her in bra and panties. Just then she noticed that we were standing in front of a huge window and went, 'OHMIGAWD!'

'The quicker you're naked, the quicker it's over with,' Jenny said.

It took her for ever to unhook her bra and slip it off her arms. She hesitated before pulling down her panties. When she was naked and Jenny had all her clothes, Jenny and Karin left the two of us standing on the landing, giggling as they walked off. I was silently counting to fifty again, my hearing super-sensitive to any sounds. Ashley was almost hyperventilating. I finally reached fifty and started down the hall to my room.

Ashley just stood there.

'Come on, Ashley, *come on*!' I pleaded.

She broke out of her trance and trotted after me. We got to the door and I knocked.

'Who is it?'

'It's Sloane and Ashley. May we come in?'

'What will you do for it, Sloane and Ashley?'

'*Anything*, Karin, *please* let us in.'

'Will you stand in front of the window?'

My stomach clenched. 'Yes, if that is what you want, darling.'

The door opened and Karin and Jenny were giggling delightfully. Karin stepped back and I walked in followed immediately by Ashley. Karin walked to the window and made sure the curtains were wide open. She crooked her finger at me and I slowly walked to the window. She made sure that I was right in the middle of it and facing out and then walked back and sat on the couch.

'How long do I have to stand here, Karin?' I asked.

'Until Jeremy calls me, darling. I want him and any of his friends to get a *good* look at you. And anyone else who looks over here.'

I started squirming, thinking about those guys seeing me.

'What's going on here?' Jenny asked.

'Well, I decided that I wanted to show my honey off so we started today. After she took a bath I had her dry off in front of the window and called a guy I know to have him look at our window. So my little honey is drying off and five guys are watching her. It was so much *fun* knowing that *they* know what she looks like naked. So we'll be doing more of that and probably some other things too. I just haven't thought of *what* for sure; I have some ideas.'

'Guys? Really?' Jenny looked a bit disgusted, being a die-hard butch.

Karin shrugged. 'She may not like it now, but I think

in time she'll become used to it. After a number of people have seen her naked, what problem is one more?'

Jenny shook her head. 'You called a *guy* to have him look at her naked? Are you *crazy*?'

'It isn't *me* they're seeing. Sloane, turn around and show your ass to the window.'

I turned, happy to just be showing my ass. I mean, everyone has one, right? I was starting to justify what I was doing to myself. I knew that my rationalisation was a bad sign. I was already preparing myself mentally for other things ...

'This *is* interesting,' Jenny said. 'Can Ashley join her?'

Karin said, 'As long as she doesn't cover up any part of my slut, sure.'

Jenny said, 'Ashley, get your naked slutty ass over there. I want you to show your big tits and hairy pussy.'

Ashley looked like she might start crying. 'I don't want to, Jenny.'

'It doesn't matter *what* you want. Remember what you've already said to me. You said that you would *mind* me, didn't you, or didn't you mean that?'

They sounded like Karin and me.

Ashley mumbled, 'I sorta did. I mean, when I saw Sloane and Karin it looked like fun, but I wasn't planning on letting *other* people see me. Especially guys. I thought, I mean I thought you meant it would be you and me and like that. Not *this*.'

147

Jenny sighed hard. 'Make up your mind, bitch. Either you're going to obey me or you aren't.'

'Can I please think about it for a few days, Jenny? This is a little *too much* right now.'

Jenny rolled her eyes. 'I'll give you *two days*, Ashley. Then you make up your mind once and for all.'

Ashley was relieved. 'Thank you, *thank you*.'

Jenny disgustedly tossed Ashley's clothes at her and I watched Ashley get dressed, wishing I could too. Once more I was the only one naked and it really made me feel self-conscious.

Karin's phone rang.

'Hi, Jeremy. You're looking again? *With binoculars?* Does she look any better? You guys aren't *fighting* over them, are you? Her ass is red because I spanked her earlier today. You want her to turn around? Sloane, face the window and smile.'

I took a deep breath and turned so my face, breasts and bush faced the window. I felt my face heating up once more.

'How many of you are there? *Seven?* That's great, Jeremy. Sure I can have her do that. Sloane, move your feet apart, please.'

I whimpered but did as Karin told me. Moving my feet apart was one of the hardest things I have ever done, because I knew I was being watched as I did it. Even embarrassed as I was, I could feel my lips sticking together and as I shifted my feet I could feel them pull slightly apart. I felt so nasty. How could I be getting excited doing this? Was I really an exhibitionist? Shouldn't it bother me so much more to be doing this with guys watching me? I mean, if my face was covered it would be so much better, but it wasn't and those guys would know who I was.

Karin on the phone: '*Oh*, you want some*th*ing else? Sure, I can have her do that too. Sloane, pull a chair up to the window, sit down and spread your legs.'

'Karin, *please* don't make me ...'

'I won't "make" you, darling, but you *do* love me, don't you? If you love me you'll do *any*thing for me, won't you?'

Why did she always play the guilt trip with me? If I did what she asked or told me, I loved her, and of course I did, but did it have to include me being humiliated? Why couldn't we just be a couple and do things together? While I was internally conflicted, I knew that in the end, if she persisted, I was going to end up doing what she wanted anyway, so why was I fighting it? I moved over to my desk and pulled my chair to the centre of the window. I sat down and lifted my feet to the window sill and with a strained smile to my honey I let my legs fall open.

I looked down and could see my lips swollen and red, wet and puffy. How could I be *aroused* by this? Was there something wrong with me?

I slid my ass forward until it was just on the edge of the chair and moved my feet apart at a smile from Karin.

'Wonderful, darling, just *wonder*ful. How is *that*, Jeremy? Oh yeah? So be *happy* today, Jeremy. I'm sure you haven't seen that many real live naked girls before so be happy. Bye, dude.'

I just sat there, stupidly, on display, mortified, humiliated, embarrassed and, to my confusion, excited. In a slight reflection from the window, I could see Jenny and Ashley watching me. They must think I am a slut or a whore. After about twenty minutes when I was sure hundreds of people saw me, Karin finally relented and let me move away from the window.

'Well,' Karin said, satisfied, '*that* was *fun*, wasn't it?'

'I still can't believe she did it,' Jenny said, 'that guys – *eww*.'

'It's just a *game*. And it's going to be fun to play it, right, Sloane?'

I didn't say a word.

'Sloane, it's just tits, an ass and a pussy. You don't have anything *special*. We all pretty much look the same and for a guy just seeing it is a big thrill. Think of how much enjoyment you've given to the student body. *That* should make you feel pretty special.'

I blurted, 'They've seen me and I have no idea *who* they are! It could be the guy next to me in class or anyone I pass on campus.'

'So it would be *easier* if you knew them?' she asked.

'I didn't say that, it's just ...'

'It's just a *body*, Sloane. Nothing more and nothing less. What's in a *body*? Don't be so upset about it. It didn't hurt you a bit and from watching you myself it sure did look like it was enjoyable.'

I flushed bright red as she reminded me of how my body reacted. There was little conversation after that and shortly Jenny and Ashley left. I was still naked. Karin came over to me and kissed me hotly.

'You have no idea how *much* your little show turned me on, Sloane. Get the strap-on.'

As I went to do as commanded, Karin stripped off her clothes. When I turned with her strap-on in my hand she was gloriously, stunningly naked. I walked up to her and touched her cheek with my free hand and everything was all right. Karin bent over and kissed me passionately. Our bodies pressed into one another and heat flashed through me like a spontaneous combustion. *This was so right even if almost everyone else would think it so wrong.* She took the strap-on and slipped into it and pushed me back onto her bed. My legs opened wide and Karin slid between them; quickly she was at my pussy hole and up inside me. She thrust deep inside me and then began the hip movement that told me it was going to be a loving session, not a fuck, *but lovemaking*. My legs rose up and crossed her back just above her ass and she lay on top

151

of me with our breasts pressed together. And she made love to me just like I always wanted it, slow, steady and deep inside me. We kissed each other hungrily, panted on each other. My hips rose to meet each thrust, wanting to take her whole body inside. My hands clutched her ass below my crossed ankles. It was stupendous, wonderful and tender. After a long time, Karin came, her squirms, twitches and soft cries setting me off so I got off too, shortly after she started. She rolled me on my side and spooned her naked body against mine, and one hand softly held one of my breasts as we fell asleep together.

Beach Scene
Primula Bond

The weather's lousy this morning. The sky's a ceiling,
bending under the weight of an overflowing bath. The
surf licks the beach suspiciously, as if it tastes nasty. But
the sand near the high dunes is still glowing pinky-yellow
from yesterday's sunshine. So what if I fancy a skinny
dip? There's nowt but a couple of seagulls watching me.
And no one else gives a toss.

If that sounds sulky then damn right I'm in a sulk. The
weekend's properly trashed. Christ, it's barely started. It
was meant to be a girlie weekend, just me and Jackie. I
needed, need, to unwind, and this is the best place to do
it. Jackie welcomes me to her little seaside place whenever
I need to shake off the woes of city life.

And last night the two of us were perfectly happy
sitting out in the unseasonal warmth of Jackie's garden,
wrapped in pashminas as her fire pit crackled. We'd eaten

one of her amazing 'snacks', which are really gourmet meals that she rustles up while I'm perched on the stool in her kitchen, giving her chapter and verse of my latest disaster. We were about to open a second bottle. Jackie was all ears. I've come all the way from London to have a proper moan, and she's always prepared. She's brilliant at listening, understanding, murmuring all the right things to stroke my battered ego, then she declares yet again that this Simon bloke is a total waste of space, that it can't possibly be my fault I've caught him twice in my bed with some slapper from the office. Actually the same slapper.

How can it possibly be my fault? Thank God for Jackie. She's a really good friend. No one else would put up with me the way she does, be so patient with me while I bang on. I always float away from an evening or weekend with her feeling that actually my life's OK. While hers is pretty dull, bless her.

Or so I thought. I still can't quite believe my own eyes. What I heard, and saw, last night. That's why I had to get away from the cottage just now. I had to run down here to the cold, stony beach. Maybe the brisk wind, choppy waves and ceaseless horizon will clear my mind a little.

Because it feels as if everything I knew about Jackie has been shaken up like a kaleidoscope and I feel utterly betrayed.

So, anyway. The Sauvignon Blanc from Jackie's cellar

was beading nicely at the rim and I was unscrewing the top with that satisfying twisty sound a wine bottle makes, when a car screeched up the narrow street to the gate. It must have woken the whole village. It was well past closing time by now.

The front door crashed open, banged shut, and footsteps clacked across the old tiled floor. Jackie jumped in her chair and blushed scarlet. I assumed she was as scared as I was, some intruder barging in like that. A light-footed intruder, admittedly, but – and then some woman I've never seen before sauntered through onto the lawn as if she owned the place.

I gripped the arms of the garden chair, ready to scream at her to get lost, to protect poor Jackie, but to my astonishment instead of waving a big stick at the woman Jackie leapt to her feet, rushed across the grass and kissed her. *Smack on the lips.*

The woman's mouth lingered on Jackie's, leaving a smear of red lipstick on Jackie's unpainted lips, and they went on staring at each other, each holding on to the other as if they were saving each other's lives.

'I'm not intruding, am I, Jackie darling?' the woman asked in a low, sexy, smoker's voice. Like she cared. 'I just had to see you before I go back to Paris.'

'Oh God, I'm so glad you did. I was feeling so desperate about you going back home. I know it's only for a few days but –'

155

I cleared my throat to stop Jackie's hysterical twittering. I'd never heard her voice flutter like that, so high-pitched and excited.

'Oh, sorry, Lola!' Jackie squealed, her hand flying up to her cheek as if she was in some kind of amateur stage production. She moved closer to the newcomer. Kind of pressed herself against her, and I saw the other woman's arm snake round Jackie's little waist as they turned towards me. 'This is Suzette.'

There was an electrified pause. I realised I was supposed to know who this woman was. Jackie must have told me about her. And as usual I wasn't listening.

'Hi,' I managed to mutter, but it was all that was needed because they turned back towards each other and started chattering away about people and places and plans I'd never heard of.

I was tuning out of the conversation and checking my empty inbox when Jackie said in a kind of simpering schoolgirl voice, 'Stay, Suzette, can't you? Just one night?'

Suzette stared at her, stroking Jackie's blonde hair back behind her ear. God, I could have punched her. Both of them.

'How can I resist that gorgeous face? Of course I'll stay, *chérie*. I can probably find the Eurostar around here somewhere, *n'est-ce pas?*'

Jackie giggled as if this Suzette had said the funniest thing in the world. She clapped her hands. 'That's settled then. It'll be such fun! You two have a little chat while I get another glass!'

'I didn't know Devon was on the way to Paris,' I muttered, as Suzette lowered herself gracefully on to Jackie's abandoned chair and crossed one slim brown leg over the other. Her floaty white skirt rode up over her thigh and a silver chain twinkled round her ankle. 'This is a bit of a detour, surely?'

'Oh, I'll go to the ends of the earth for a good time,' replied Suzette calmly, tossing a handful of peanuts into her mouth. 'Especially if my Jackie's there.'

Jackie returned with the glass and some wicked desserts. The garden was lit only by the moon, the lights from the house and the fairy lights and lanterns dotted round the patio. It all looked seductive and magical but, despite the second bottle of wine slipping down a treat and the comfortable murmur of female friends, the spark of the evening had gone for me.

I sat for a few more minutes, virtually ignored and observing the way Jackie practically bowed down and worshipped this Suzette creature. There was no need for such craven adoration, and I would tell her so just as soon as this interloper had gone. It demeaned Jackie, made her look grovelling. But I had to admit that Princess Suzette was, is, pretty fucking cool. Glossy black hair expensively cut, huge brown eyes immaculately made up, tiny hands and feet dazzlingly bejewelled, and those elegant white clothes that seemed to slip off her limbs as she talked.

She was so impossibly beautiful and elegant that she made Jackie look like an over-eager Bo-Peep and me – well, I felt like a jumpy mare.

'I'm off to bed,' I said abruptly, just as I suspect they were realising their rudeness and about to turn the spotlight onto me at last. 'You too obviously have loads to catch up.'

They made token noises of protest but I was so pissed off that I stomped into the house without waiting to hear what they had to say.

But, guys, it all gets worse. Much worse. Jackie's cottage is cute, if you're in a good mood, or poky, if you're in a strop, and you can hear every creaking floorboard, every rustling blackbird in the roof.

And in the night I was awoken by noises. Not out on the lawn, or downstairs. There was soft whispering coming from inside the house, from inside Jackie's bedroom a few steps down the landing, female laughter choking off, and then the silence prised open by a couple of long moans. What the fuck? I pushed open Jackie's door to tell her to shut up, turn the radio or the porno movie off.

And I still haven't got over what I saw.

It wasn't the radio. The CD was simply playing some very quiet jazz. Nor was Jackie alone. Suzette was in the bedroom with her. In the bed, actually. They were practically naked, and kind of wriggling, but even so I still thought that they were tickling, or play-fighting. But no. They were making out. They were about to fuck each other and I was about to see what women can do to each other.

Yeah, yeah, I know, you're all saying how on earth could I have missed all that steamy body language, the electricity sizzling between them from the moment the Princess arrived? Well, with all my problems, I just did. I had no idea, in all the years I've known her, that Jackie had experimented with gay sex, or was that way inclined – hell, she's never come on to *me*! And I certainly hadn't dug, probably because I was so furious that she had turned up at all, and because they were so soft of girlie and cute with each other, that this Suzette was some kind of predatory lesbian. But there they both were, in all their Technicolor 3D glory, one pale girl, one dark, their pouty lips locked together, tongues glistening as they pushed in and out of each other's mouths, bodies moving slowly and dreamily as they kissed, skin and limbs and hair flickering in the scented candles Jackie had placed all over the window sills, the dresser, the floor, voices only moaning now –

As I watched, Jackie turned and got down on all fours on top of her huge patchwork quilt, her bottom perking up in the air, and Suzette, wearing just French knickers, knelt behind her. Jackie was arching her back. I never realised how big her tits were. They hung down like huge luscious fruit, dark nipples pointing so hard that they made sharp shadows against her skin, and to my horror my stomach lurched at the sight.

Suzette's hands were on Jackie's ass, stroking, slapping, and then she pulled Jackie's pussy open. Jackie swayed her bottom to and fro, pushing it at her princess, and slowly Suzette bent down and kissed Jackie's butt, kissed it all over, her hands still tugging open those butt cheeks, and then her tongue snaked out, long and wet, and swept it up Jackie's crack. Jackie moaned loudly, her throat arched with pleasure and she pushed her fanny hard back into Suzette's face.

I leaned in the doorway, holding my breath. My heart was banging in my ribs and I could feel the hot push of excitement springing between my legs. God, I was so embarrassed at them, at myself. I didn't want them to know I was watching.

Suzette drew back, her big mouth wet with Jackie's cunt juice. And then, I'm sure of it, before diving back into Jackie's cunt like a cat to start lapping, I'm sure she winked straight at me.

Oh, it's all so gross, and that lecherous little wink was enough to wake me up and have me scarpering back to my bed and stuffing the pillow over my ears.

And to make it all so much worse I'm stuck here at

least until I can get one of them to run me to the station so I can get back to civilisation and away from all this selfish madness.

At least out here on the beach I don't have to listen to them going at it like knives all morning. Because believe me, they did. Until the early hours, anyway. They were asleep when I tiptoed out just now. And yeah, I'm jealous, OK? Jackie's *my* friend. We were at college together, knowing each other's secrets long before this upstart Suzette came along. And no, I don't fancy her. But how long is it since I was fucked loudly enough to wake the neighbours?

I start running. Get this aggro out of me. The waves seem to have calmed down a little and are glinting in a steely slice of sunshine. It's still early morning. Shoes and jeans off, toes gripping damp sand. Jumper off, and my skin shivers and shrinks. It'll hurt, that bitter cold, but I'm that angry and frustrated. T-shirt off. I hate wet fabric sticking to me.

My nipples tighten in the cold, poking out like hard red berries. Don't think about Jackie's big dangling tits, Suzette's tongue on her pussy, probably those big lips sucking on Jackie's tits later on in the night. I force my legs to run through the rolling weight of the sea until I scream and throw myself forwards.

In seconds I'm totally numb. I'll probably die from the cold, then they'll be sorry. I swim back, ears rushing and eyes stinging, feet scraping on the shingle as I stagger out. My clothes seem miles away, and the stones are digging into my bare feet. I can hardly see through the salt in my eyes and the hair stuck across my face.

'I didn't have you down as a nutcase.'

I stop dead, wind and spray whipping round me, furiously wiping my eyes. Suzette is there, in some kind of velvety poncho, and she's flapping a towel at me like a pair of wings. Of course in all my fury I'd forgotten to grab a towel.

'Oh, leave me alone,' I gasp, bending for my clothes. She kicks them into a heap. 'Go back to your hot little lover.'

'She'll keep. She's fast asleep. Now. This is what you need. Come on. Out of the breeze.'

My teeth are chattering now, my whole body shaking. 'I'm not your little Jackie, you know. You can't order me about.'

Suzette walks into the shelter of the dunes and sits down in the sand, still holding out the towel. I really want that towel round me now. I have to follow her, if only just to keep moving, and I feel fucking stupid. Suzette looks beautiful even in her baggy top and jeans. She has red lipstick on. She watches me.

'Fantastic body you have, Lola. Who knew? If it wasn't for the pasty sulky city face you could be a lovely mermaid.'

'We can't all be sultry French princesses.' I have no choice now. I grab at the towel and plonk down on the

162

damp sand with my back to her. 'So which body do you prefer, Jackie's or mine?'

'Don't be an arsehole. You don't give a toss what I think about you, but if you're going to prance about in full view of the village street butt-naked, people are going to look, aren't they? I'm not the only one who's seen you this morning, I can tell you!' Suzette rubs my shoulders briskly like some kind of nanny. 'Lucky I'm not some randy bloke passing by. He'd be down here on the beach fucking that mood right out of you in five minutes. Those gorgeous breasts are enough to warm the cockles, I can tell you. Not to mention the see-through knickers, that cute little snatch. Nicely waxed, girlfriend –'

'I'm not your fucking girlfriend!' I try to stand up, but my legs are weak from the cold. This woman is making my hair stand on end, but I try to hide my confusion with an angry shrug.

'Whoa, touchy. Just being friendly!'

'I'm not so desperate that I need to steal Jackie's friends, thanks.'

'Who said anything about stealing?'

'Oh, stop messing with me.' I allow her to rub at my tangled hair. 'I admit I was a bit stupid going in the water, but I was so, you know, so *furious*!'

'You mean jealous?'

'You wish. No. I'm not a lesbian. You're welcome to all that.'

Suzette starts rubbing my arms now. 'Jackie never told me she had such a sexy friend.'

'And Miss Jackie never told me she was into women.'

'Look at you, Lola. All hunched up and tense. No wonder Jackie doesn't tell you things.'

'If she wants hunched up and tense, she's got it. I want to get dressed.'

'Not until I've massaged you into some kind of calmness. I'm a professional masseuse, didn't Jackie tell you? It's best to work on you now, after all that vigorous exercise.' Suzette's hands move up my arms and onto my spine. 'It's not fair on poor Jackie, not to mention fucking rude. So if you still won't relax after I've finished with you, you can fuck off back to London and give Jackie a break.'

I'm half warm, where her hands are, and half cold, where the air is sneaking in under the towel.

'You're the one who can fuck off.'

Suzette's hands smooth over my back until the blood is simmering with warmth, and they work on up to my jaw. She must be some kind of hypnotist as well as a masseuse, because I'm in a trance now, and that's when Suzette twists my neck and there's a loud crack. I'm about to yell blue murder, but then it's like she's lifted a motorbike helmet off my skull.

'Still feel like being rude to someone who could break your neck?' She chuckles softly.

I'm too dizzy to speak. Suzette's hands start working

faster, unzipping the tension in my body with a combination of pain and pleasure. Her fingers tread up and down my spine and then the towel is slipping down and her fingers are counting up and between my ribs. The towel falls right to my waist and my tits swell with the new shock of cold on the surface of my skin, while underneath my body is boiling with heat and life. Suzette's hands come round to the front and she presses my breasts softly together, making my nipples pop out hard again

She stops, and I am furious at the slump of disappointment in my chest. 'Hot work, this. If you can sit there naked, I don't see why I shouldn't.'

I hear her pulling her poncho off over her head. I can feel heavy velvet swishing against my skin, and she must have nothing on underneath, because there are her small breasts squashing into my back. Lola laughs, her breath warm on my neck. Now she's brazen. She's no longer concentrating on my bones. She's openly squeezing my tits, no question, the nipples trapped and pulled between her fingers, singing with pleasure at the cold breeze and her fingers flicking hot pleasure from them.

My pussy tightens, then melts open. Oh God, I'm liking this. There's a woman fondling my tits sending desire right through me and, yeah, I like it.

Suzette rubs my nipples between her finger and thumb until they're rigid and aching with longing but she's also rubbing her own nipples against my bare back, so that I can feel them scraping across my skin. She rocks me with her and I watch her hands rubbing and lifting my tits and weighing them, feel her grinding her groin against me and sure enough now I'm getting horny.

I'm vaguely aware that the tide's coming in. We might have to move further up the beach, and we certainly ought to get into some kind of hiding place. The seagulls are screeching like someone calling across the dunes. I swivel round to face Suzette, not sure what to do next. She lies back and starts to undo her jeans, but I want to do it. Her tits are much smaller than mine, but they are firm and jutting skywards, nipples just begging to be licked. Oh God, did I just say that?

She looks small and helpless for a moment, only pretending, but it's enough. I lean over and yank her trousers off, pulling her pants away with them. She is waxed totally naked, all the better to tempt you with, and the dark slit is parted, already wet.

My tits are dangling in her face as I bend over her, and she pulls me down and nips one nipple between her teeth and holds fast. I hang over her for a minute while she suckles me, then she's edging her fingers under my wet knickers and inside my own slit, opening it, tickling the tenderness, and I can hear my juice wet against Suzette's fingers. She probes, searching for my clit, and I can't help it, I have to spread my legs wider to expose it for her. And I want my tits in her face. Her tongue slicks across one nipple then the other and I start moaning. No one can hear, she's sucking and it's so good – but what about her pleasure?

I want to feel her. I push my fingers into her cunt and she bucks sharply. I push my fingers in and out of her like a cock, feeling her cunt grasping to keep me inside, and I want to be rough with her. I want to be a cock. It's warm in there and so wet as my fingers fuck her.

Suddenly Suzette tips herself sideways, rolling us both so that we're face to face, working our fingers into each other, my nipples tingling deliciously from her lips and teeth. But I want to taste those lips and teeth, and her cat's tongue slides inside my mouth and we're sucking on each other, bodies writhing with the friction, her mouth soft like sex lips.

Suzette hooks her leg over me and we push our fingers and groins together, pussy lips spread open to surrender the redness, kissing like lovers, and now the heat's rising. Every time she flicks my clit or thrusts further inside, I do the same to her and she jerks and now the tip of my climax is slicing through me, Suzette's fingers still flicking and pounding, and my cunt contracts and I come in waves like the tide, flowing then crashing, and when I hear Suzette gasp and scream I want to shout out loud with triumph.

We're lying there, panting, and I roll over to stare at the dazzling white sky, but someone's standing between me and the sun.

'When you've finished seducing my lover, Lola, look who's come all this way to see you.'

I sit up, scrabbling for the towel, but Suzette just lies there smiling lazily up at Jackie, splayed out naked for all to see.

'Hey, Jacks,' I stammer, staring at the sand. I can tell she's livid. 'Your Suzette's something else, isn't she?'

'And so are you, Lola girl.' The last time I saw him he was thrusting his dick into that slapper from the office. 'I didn't think you had it in you.'

'So there was a randy bloke passing by, after all. Better and better.' Suzette stands up, stretching. She touches Jackie, who shakes her off.

Simon doesn't move. He can't believe his eyes.

'You've had a wasted journey,' I tell him. 'I've found something else I like a whole lot better.'

Suzette puts her arm round my waist. I pull Jackie over, and reluctantly she joins us. She's upset. But we'll sort her out.

'You give him hell, girl,' says Suzette. 'But I don't know about a wasted journey. He's tasty. Well hung, I'll bet.'

The three of us look Simon up and down. Up and down.

'I've flattened his tyres,' Jackie says, starting to laugh.

'Then we've got all weekend,' I say.

And the three sirens walk up to the randy bloke, surround him and push him down onto the sand.